Oranges and Murder

'Lord James. Called after your old man, weren't you?'

Joey has always known that Curly the coster isn't his real father, but he can't believe that he is the son of a lord as the other boys say. Anyway, he's too busy to think about it much. He's planning to set up on his own as a market trader, and he dreams of a red-haired girl called Annie.

But when he meets Quill Quennell, the screever, a man who will write letters for anyone who can pay, and who seems to know something about Joey's past, Joey begins to wonder if there is something in the gossip after all. Then Quennell is murdered and Joey has to go into hiding, afraid for his own life. If the screever was killed to keep him quiet, what was the secret he knew? And can Joey find out the truth before it is too late?

Alison Prince was born in London and at 17 she won a scholarship to the Slade School of Art. She was Head of Art at a London comprehensive school until she married and had three children, when she started writing. At first it was journalism and then children's television, where she wrote several series including *Trumpton*, and appeared on *Jackanory*. This led to a publisher proposing she write her first book and she has been writing ever since—over thirty-six books for adults and chil̲ ̲ ̲ ̲ ̲ ̲ ̲ ̲ ̲ ̲ farm in Suffolk for eight years and th̲ ̲ ̲ ̲ ̲ ̲ ̲ ̲ ̲ ̲ ̲ ̲ and now lives on the Isle o̲ ̲ ̲ ̲ ̲ ̲ ̲ ̲ ̲ ̲ ̲ and loved since childhood. ̲ ̲ ̲ ̲ ̲ ̲ ̲ ̲ ̲ ̲ ̲ Children's Fiction Award a̲ ̲ ̲ ̲ ̲ ̲ ̲ ̲ ̲ ̲ ̲ ̲ Smarties Award. *Oranges a̲ ̲ ̲ ̲ ̲ ̲ ̲ ̲ ̲ ̲ ̲* or Oxford University Press.

Oranges and Murder

Other Oxford books

Hero
Catherine R. Johnson

The Coldest Winter
Elizabeth Lutzeier

Bound for America
Elizabeth Lutzeier

Hold My Hand and Run
Margaret McAllister

War Song
James Riordan

Oranges and Murder

Alison Prince

OXFORD
UNIVERSITY PRESS

OXFORD
UNIVERSITY PRESS

Great Clarendon Street, Oxford OX2 6DP

Oxford University Press is a department of the University of Oxford.
It furthers the University's objective of excellence in research, scholarship,
and education by publishing worldwide in

Oxford New York
Auckland Bangkok Buenos Aires
Cape Town Chennai Dar es Salaam Delhi Hong Kong Istanbul
Karachi Kolkata Kuala Lumpur Madrid Melbourne Mexico City Mumbai
Nairobi São Paulo Shanghai Singapore Taipei Tokyo Toronto

With an associated company in Berlin

Oxford is a registered trade mark of Oxford University Press
in the UK and in certain other countries

Copyright © Alison Prince 2001

The moral rights of the author have been asserted

Database right Oxford University Press (maker)

First published 2001
First published in this edition 2002

All rights reserved. No part of this publication may be reproduced,
stored in a retrieval system, or transmitted, in any form or by any means,
without the prior permission in writing of Oxford University Press.
Within the UK, exceptions are allowed in respect of any fair
dealing for the purpose of research or private study, or criticism or
review, as permitted under the Copyright, Designs and Patents Act 1988,
or in the case of reprographic reproduction in accordance with
the terms of the licences issued by the Copyright Licensing Agency.
Enquiries concerning reproduction outside these terms and in other
countries should be sent to the Rights Department, Oxford University Press,
at the above address.

This book is sold subject to the condition that it shall not, by way of trade or
otherwise, be lent, re-sold, hired out or otherwise circulated without
the publisher's prior consent in any form of binding or cover other than that in
which it is published and without a similar condition including this condition
being imposed on the subsequent purchaser.

British Library Cataloguing in Publication Data available

ISBN 0 19 275264 2

1 3 5 7 9 10 8 6 4 2

Typeset by AFS Image Setters Ltd, Glasgow

Printed in Great Britain by
Cox & Wyman Ltd, Reading, Berkshire

20089235
MORAY COUNCIL
LIBRARIES &
INFORMATION SERVICES
JC Y

1

'Come on, Joey.' Poll was shaking me by the shoulder. 'It's gone five. Time to get up.'

She'd lit a candle, but it was pitch dark outside and the room was cold, even though it smelt fuggy with the six of us sleeping in it. I was warm and cosy under the blanket I shared with Bobby, and it would have been nice to stay there.

'Come on,' Poll said again. 'Your pa won't like it if you're late.'

That was putting it mildly. When Curly didn't like something, you got a clip round the ear, and lucky if it was nothing worse. So I got up and started putting my clothes on. I wondered, not for the first time, why Poll had said, 'Your pa.' Curly wasn't my pa, and everyone knew it. I didn't even look like him. My hair was sandy-coloured, not black and curly like his. That's where he got his nickname, from his hair. Most costers have nicknames. My ma's called Tin-head Poll, from the time when Curly hit her with the frying pan. I can't have been more than six, but I still remember it. She didn't even stagger, just took the pan out of his hand and hung it on the wall by the bit of string through its handle, and Curly sat down with his head in his hands. I stopped calling her Ma when I started working on the barrow two years ago. I was eight then, and it made me feel grown up to call her Poll.

Anyway, I took a lantern and went out, eating a bit of bread and jam. Frost was sparkling on the cobbles, but it

1

wasn't cold in the stable. There were a dozen or so donkeys and ponies in there under the low roof, and although the place looked a bit ramshackle, there was plenty of straw, and the animals kept it warm. I got on with harnessing Daisy. She was quite small as donkeys go, but a willing worker. I'd just backed her between the shafts of the barrow when Curly came in.

'Time you'd finished that,' he said in his grating, husky voice. It had cracked through shouting his wares along the streets for so long, and he depended on me to make most of the noise these days. I held Daisy while he climbed on the driving box and gathered up the reins. He looked a lot bigger than the donkey, up there with his jacket tight across his bulky shoulders and his cap pulled down over one eye.

'Giddup,' he said, and Daisy started forward. I blew the lantern out and latched the stable door then followed him, walking beside the barrow. I knew better than to try and climb up before I was asked. Some days, we were halfway to the market before he'd let me up—he said he didn't believe in kids growing up spoiled. But this morning was pretty good; we'd only just turned out into the Minories when he stopped and said, 'Come on, then.' I put a foot on the wheel and scrambled up beside him.

It was a long way from our patch in Whitechapel to Covent Garden, but most of the costers reckoned it was worth going there for their stock. It was by far the biggest market, and farmers came in from miles around with their produce. Some of them travelled all night. There was stuff from the docks as well—lemons and oranges and pomegranates, even grapes and pineapples sometimes, though they were too fancy for us.

The sky was still dark when we got there, but the big gas lamps lit the place up. I loved the Garden—I still do. There's so much of everything, great piles of cabbages and turnips stacked on the steps of the theatre and spilling out of every doorway along the side streets, together with leeks and broccoli and bundles of carrots and celery and brown onions plaited together by their tops. And the smell of the fruit made my mouth water—it still does, though I'm handling the stuff every day.

Curly was a tough haggler over prices. He bought for several other costers as well as himself, because it was cheaper to get a big lot and split it between them. My job was to load the barrow. Sounds easy, but there's an art to stacking stuff properly so the customer can see a bit of everything. And there's only a narrow board round the edge to stop things falling off, so you have to make sure nothing will work loose through jolting over the cobbles. When I'd finished, I dug out the rest of the bread Poll had given me and sat on the shaft, eating it. Curly was in the pub with his mates, sorting out the money.

We went back a different way, across the Strand and down towards the river. I didn't know where we were heading, and Curly wasn't talking. He turned the donkey down Swan Lane, with the walls of the warehouses close on both sides, and we came out by the river. He put the reins in my hand and said, 'I got some business to see to.'

I watched him set off with the river on his right, but then he disappeared through a gap between the buildings on the other side, just across from where a flight of steps leads down to the water. I could guess where he'd gone. Red Jack lived somewhere round here, people said, in a place called Black Raven Alley. And to us kids, Red Jack was all the old stories of giants and kings rolled into one. He was supposed to have amazing riches hidden away behind those sooty walls, and there were rumours that he was in with a gang of smugglers who ran stuff in through the London docks under the very noses of the Customs

3

men. Maybe they were just tales—it was difficult to tell, because if grown-ups noticed you were listening when they talked about Red Jack, you got sent off pretty sharp. But I did know Curly was renting his barrow from him. A lot of the costers did, until they got the money together to buy an outfit of their own. Curly never had any money, though. He earned a fair bit, specially with me helping, but Poll had a hard job to get a few bob out of him before he went off to the pub, and what with the beer and the games of three-up, he nearly always came home skint.

I sat there for a few more minutes, then Curly came back and we set off again, past the north side of London Bridge and then down towards Billingsgate. 'I'll get a bit of fish if the price is right,' he said.

To be honest, I've never liked Billingsgate Market. Fish is all right once it's fried, but the smell of it raw turns me up, specially if it's a bit off—and it always is by the end of the day. And in the market, some of it's still alive and twitching, never mind the eels sliding around in their open boxes. I wouldn't tell anyone I'm squeamish about it because they'd laugh, but I didn't mind when Curly said I'd to stay and look after the stock while he took a look round. He went off with the tin dish we kept under the driving box, and I gave Daisy a couple of bruised apples I'd picked up in the Garden, then sat on the wall and looked at the river.

The tide was out, so a shoal of mud reached from the wall to the water. There were people wading knee-deep in it, feeling with their feet for bits of coal or old iron—anything they could sell. Mudlarks, we called them, but it wasn't much of a lark, not really. A kid drowned there last year. Slipped and lost his footing, and once you're down in that black slime, you're lucky if you get up again.

I sat there watching, and felt glad I was a coster, with my feet dry and warm in good boots. Whatever else we have or don't have, us costers pride ourselves on our boots. One of the mudlarks straightened up to drop something into the sack he carried—and he saw me and waved. 'Wotcher, Lord James!' he shouted. 'Taking it easy?'

It was Lucky Luke. He'd slipped once, but they got to him in time. I hadn't seen him for ages. A lot of the boys used to call me Lord James, but most of them stopped after I cut up rough about it. There was some stupid story going round that I was the son of a toff or something, and I wasn't having that.

Lucky was standing there, grinning.

'Where've you been?' I shouted.

'Living in the old boathouse.' He waved an arm up-river. 'It ain't bad.'

I knew the place he meant. It stood on a wooden jetty, but half the roof had gone and it was falling to pieces. I took a breath to say something else, but Curly appeared, with the tin dish full of whiting. 'Hold that,' he said, so I had to climb on the box with the dish on my lap, and when I looked back at Lucky he'd turned away to reach down into the water for something else.

I thought about him as Daisy started up the lane to Lower Thames Street. We used to play together when we were little kids, though he was a bit older than me. His father was away at sea, then news came that his ship had gone down—and soon after that, Lucky's mother and his little brother died of scarlet fever, about the same time my sister Jenny did. I never knew where he got to. The other kids said he'd gone to his grandma, but I didn't know where.

'Who was you talking to?' Curly asked—and when I told him, he shook his head. 'You don't want to go around with scum like that,' he said.

'I don't go around with him,' I mumbled, and felt a bit ashamed, because I'd meant to say that Lucky wasn't

5

scum, only I was too scared of Curly to argue with him. Luck was a funny thing. With a different throw of the dice, it could have been me down there in the mud, and Lucky Luke riding through the streets in good boots.

'Long as you don't,' said Curly. 'Us costers got our pride.'

And I just nodded and kept my mouth shut.

I started shouting the wares as soon as we were back in Whitechapel. I had a voice like a canary, being only ten, and my sandy-coloured hair helped, too. Poll said it made me look honest, but that's a load of rubbish. Some of the worst twisters I know have got fair hair and a straight pair of blue eyes—but whatever it was, I always did well at selling. 'Fresh red apples!' I'd sing out. 'Sweet oranges, two a penny!' And if the customers smiled at me, I always smiled back. They like that.

By mid-afternoon we'd sold the whole barrow-load except for a couple of cabbages and a few leeks, and when we got home, Curly nodded at them and said, 'You can have those.' If there was a lot left, he'd keep it to sell the next day, but when there wasn't much, he let me sell it myself and keep what I made on it. All the coster boys worked that way, for 'bunts' as we called it. So I unharnessed Daisy and rubbed her down and fed her, then went off out again with the leeks and cabbages in a shallow basket, (we always called them 'shallows'), the leather strap round my neck.

This was the best time of the day. I felt like a proper person when I was out on my own, with nobody telling me what to do. I walked up to the street market. The daylight was fading and most of the stalls were packing up, but the butcher's shop was still open in a blaze of red and white under its row of gas lamps, and I could smell chestnuts roasting, and a meaty whiff from the pie stall. A barefoot girl a bit younger than me was trying to sell the last of her violets, but she wasn't having much luck. She looked at me as I passed and shrugged, and I gave her a smile, trying to remember her name. She used to be a friend of Jenny's. Rose, that was it. Red Rose, on account of her mop of hair, bright as new carrots.

'Good leeks and cabbages!' I sang out. 'All fresh and lovely!' I got no takers for a bit, then a woman stopped and looked. 'Last ones left, lady,' I said. 'Beautiful leeks, white as milk they are.'

'How much d'you want for them?' she asked.

I could see she was the bargaining sort—her thin mouth told me that—so I asked her a halfpenny more than I wanted, and settled on twopence for the lot, which was good money. 'You drive a hard bargain, lady,' I told her while she pushed the stuff into her basket, and she gave a little nod, pleased with herself.

Rose had caught up with me, and I gave her a quick wink and said to the woman, 'She's my sister. Twopence halfpenny the violets, clear 'em up? Smell how sweet they are—fresh picked this morning.'

'Ought to be threepence,' said Rose.

'Absolute nonsense,' the woman said. 'I'll give you twopence, and that's more than they're worth.'

'Done,' said Rose quickly.

Neither of us laughed until the woman had gone. We walked on past the smoked haddock stall and the woman who sold sweets and a haggard-looking man who was peddling ink and paper, and Rose said, 'Great when you've sold all your stock, isn't it. I hate it when there's flowers left over, all shrivelling up.'

'I know what you mean,' I said. She'd changed since the days when she and Jenny used to skip over a rope one of them turned, the other end tied to a lamp-post. She used

7

to be a chubby little kid, but she was thin now, and her face had that determined look, like a proper grown-up though she can't have been more than nine.

She caught me looking at her. 'My pa died,' she said as if she had to explain. 'On the docks. He got crushed between two crane-loads.'

'I didn't know,' I said. My face turned red because I couldn't find any words. I understood now about the bare feet and the torn draggled skirt. When a man died, his family had a hard time. I stopped at a coffee stall and bought a hunk of plum cake then broke it in half and gave her the bigger bit.

'Go on?' said Rose. 'You sure?' She looked amazed.

When you're only ten it makes you feel a real man to buy something for a girl, so I said, 'Of course I'm sure.'

Maybe I sounded a bit posh or something, but she giggled and said, 'Thank you, sir!' then took a big bite of the cake and laughed again, her hand to her mouth to keep the crumbs in. 'M'm, lovely,' she said, and took another bite. Then she added, 'I've got a baby brother now. His name's Stevie. He was born just after Pa died.'

'That's nice,' I said. 'You've got a sister, too, haven't you?'

Rose nodded. 'Meg. She's three.' Then her face clouded. 'Ma's not well, though. She keeps coughing all the time.'

'Perhaps she'll get better when the spring comes,' I said. Lots of people coughed in the winter.

'Hope so,' said Rose.

It was nearly dark now. We went past a stall piled with tin saucepans and another one bright with blue and yellow crockery and tea trays, then came to the Punch and Judy show. The little stage on top of the cloth-covered booth was so bright, you could forget how small Punch was. He seemed as big and red-faced as Curly in one of his moods,

8

the way he shook his stick at poor Judy and shouted at her, and the real-life dog that sat on the corner of the stage with a ruff round its neck seemed huge. Punch was shouting at Judy in the quacking voice you could hear all up and down the street. We knew how it was done, of course—the Punch and Judy man had a metal thing that he put in his mouth to make the sound come out like that. Pocky Dan, they called him, because of his face being all pitted with smallpox scars.

A big crowd of people was standing round the booth, coster boys and men as well as children and women with babies in their arms. None of them could take their eyes off what was happening on the bright little stage—and neither could I. Judy was a ghost now, rocking to and fro in a white gown, looking for her baby. Punch had killed both of them, but she didn't seem to know that. 'Where's my baby?' she wailed. 'Oh, where's my baby, my baby?'

'Poor lady,' Rose said beside me. 'Mustn't it be awful, not knowing what's happened to your kid?'

'It's only pretend,' I said.

'I know,' said Rose. But she kept on watching, and so did I, because the little, glowing world up there was just as real as the street once you entered into it, and the sadness of Judy's ghost somehow touched on a little bit of sadness deep inside me as well. Maybe inside everyone.

2

Things went on much the same until I was thirteen, and then I had my big bust-up with Curly. Bobby was ten by that time, the toughest kid you ever saw. If he was short of money he'd offer to let some bigger boy hit him on the nose for a halfpenny. Sometimes he got knocked down, but he never seemed to mind, just picked himself up and held his hand out for the money. He always got it, too. He took after Poll, I reckon. Anyway, he was helping on the barrow, and Jess and little Ernie were old enough to do a bit as well, selling walnuts and apples. As soon as coster kids can carry a small basket, they have to make themselves useful.

We weren't doing too badly, with all of us working. I thought Curly would have paid off what he owed Red Jack on the barrow, but I couldn't be sure—he didn't talk about that sort of thing, even to Poll. With Bobby and me both shouting the wares from the barrow, we'd often need another load by mid-morning, but it was a long way to go back to the Garden, and most of the stuff would be finished anyway. You could get a bit of stock from the Jewish wholesalers up in Houndsditch, but Curly wanted to go for a bigger outfit altogether. He said he was going to sell Daisy and the barrow, and buy a bigger donkey that could pull a four-wheeled cart.

I thought about it for a day or two. At thirteen, going on fourteen, I was old enough to be in business on my own. Most of the coster boys I knew had been working for themselves for a year or more, and a good few had taken

10

up with a girl, living as man and wife. Costers don't go in much for getting married—a church service costs a lot, and we never have much to do with churches anyway. So one evening when Curly seemed in a reasonable temper, I said, 'If you'd let me have Daisy and the small barrow, I could go selling on my own. I'd pay you for them a bit every week and give you a share of the takings, and you and Bobby could run the big cart.'

He looked at me with his mouth set in that obstinate way I knew so well, then said, 'You want to set up in business, boy, you go and borrow your set-up money same as the other kids do. I ain't worked all these years just to see you flaunting it round the place like Lord Muck. How d'you think I'm going to buy a bigger outfit unless I sell the one I've got?'

So that was that. He made me come with him when he took Daisy down to the 'Smithfield Racecourse', as we called it, where all the donkeys and ponies changed hands—barrows and harness, too. He tethered Daisy to the rail among the other donkeys and said, 'You stop here while I have a look round, see what I can find. Trot the donkey out if anyone shows a bit of interest—and don't take less than three quid for her. A fiver if they want the barrow as well.'

He'd be lucky, I thought. You could buy a good pony for not much more than three quid, and ponies fetched a lot more than donkeys. Specially small, rather old donkeys like Daisy. But I just nodded. There was never any point in arguing.

I perched there on the rail for a long time, watching men run up and down the muddy track, leading their animals. 'Hup-hup-hup!' they shouted. 'Mind your backs!' Nobody showed much interest in Daisy. One man looked at her teeth to see how old she was, then went off again. There was a good smell of meat pies and stewed eels from the food-stalls over by the wall, and a whiff of pea soup as well. I could have done with a bowl of that. Soup is great stuff on a raw, cold day, it warms your hands as well as your stomach. A woman passed with a basket of little red apples, shouting their price, and I smiled to myself. Who was she kidding? Anyone could see they were 'gowfs', the bitter sort that nobody wants. The trick is to mix a few of them in with the better ones.

'How's things, James?'

I turned to find Lucky Luke standing beside me, grinning that scrawny grin of his. I'd seen quite a bit of him since that time when he'd waved at me from the mud of the foreshore, because even though he wasn't a coster I somehow liked him—but he hadn't been around for a week or two.

'Not so bad,' I said. 'What've you got there?'

Lucky had a dog with him, tied by a bit of rope round its neck. Not much of a dog, just a black mongrel, but it looked quite fat and well fed.

'Got a new trade,' said Lucky, still grinning. 'Dog finding.'

I laughed. Trust Lucky to get into something like that. 'Dog kidnapping, you mean,' I said. There was a fair bit of that went on. A dog's owner would usually cough up a reward to the 'finder' who returned it. 'So what was the matter with the mudlarking?' I asked.

'Cut my foot on a bit of glass,' said Lucky, 'and it festered. Been laid up with it. So I thought I'd try something else.' He glanced at Daisy and ran a hand over one of her long ears. 'Trading her in?'

I made a face. 'Curly's moving up in the world. I hoped he'd let me have her, but he wouldn't.' Then I wondered why I was grumbling. At least Curly paid me a few pence each day for selling, plus the 'bunts' I made on my own. I had a roof over my head, and Poll always made sure there was food on the table. Lucky had nothing. 'You still in the boathouse?' I asked.

He nodded. 'It's falling down, though. I'll have to find somewhere else. Still, summer's coming. Any old place will do when the nights aren't so cold.' He grinned again. 'And a dog's nice and warm to cuddle up to. A girl would be better, but they don't seem that willing. Can't think why.'

'Don't know what they're missing,' I said. Then I saw Curly approaching, leading a big, pale-coloured jack donkey. 'Here comes trouble.'

'So it does,' said Lucky. 'I'll be off. So long, James.'

I stopped him. 'Listen, my name's Joey, right?' None of the coster boys called me James any more, and the name still made me feel vaguely uneasy.

Lucky shrugged. 'Suit yourself.'

Curly was getting closer, but I went on, 'Why James, anyway? Where did it come from?'

'Lord James,' Lucky said, grinning again. 'Called after your old man, weren't you. Some toff. So people say. See you around.' And he and his dog were gone.

I hated the new donkey on sight. He was a big, strong beast, carrying his nose high and with a cantankerous set to his ears. Curly pushed him into the line beside Daisy, and he bared his long, yellow teeth to snap at her. Curly cuffed him and said proudly, 'What d'you think of that, then?'

'I reckon you and him suit each other,' I said.

'What's that supposed to mean?' Curly was glaring, and my courage failed as it so often did.

'Well—he's strong.' I was going to add, *and bad-tempered*, but thought better of it.

'What about Daisy—you had any takers?'

'No.'

'Too busy talking to that filthy friend of yours, that's why,' Curly said. 'Don't think I didn't see you.'

13

'Lucky's all right,' I said. Being a bit dirty didn't make a person bad—and none of us were that clean, anyway.

'You arguing?' Curly aimed a slap at me, but the two donkeys were between us and he couldn't quite reach. I backed away, staring at him. *Lord James. Called after your old man, weren't you.* Suddenly, I felt a kind of pride in the name. Not that I was any kind of toff—but for the first time, I wasn't scared of Curly any more. Looking at him as he glowered across the donkeys' backs, I saw him, not as the ogre who had terrified me throughout my childhood, but as a beery-nosed man in a greasy cap, whose black eyes and strong jaw were too puffy now to be handsome.

'Yes, I'm arguing,' I said. 'And I'm going to go on arguing. So you can sell your own donkey.' I was backing away. 'And the best of luck.' Then I turned and ran.

'You come back here!' He started after me, but I was well ahead of him, and a lot faster.

After a while, well clear of Smithfield and Curly, I slowed down, shoving my hands in my pockets as I walked on. I was still hungry, but the sour taste of anger burned in my throat and I couldn't have eaten anything. I'd be in for the hiding of my life when I went home.

Why go home, then? This was the time to make a break and start up on my own. But it was easier said than done. I'd given Poll a week's money for my keep and I only had three halfpence in my pocket. I didn't even have a shallow to sell from—the one I used was Curly's property, and anyway, it was at home.

I went on up the street towards Houndsditch, heading in an automatic sort of way for Dukes Place, where Sammy Meyer ran a small wholesale business in citrus fruit.

14

Sammy was a good sort. I quite often went up there in the afternoon when I'd finished helping with the barrow, and he'd let me have some oranges to sell. We haggled a bit over the price, but he wasn't unreasonable, and he'd always credit me for any rotten fruit. But I never lied about it like some of the boys did, claiming more bad ones than there really were, and I think he knew that.

Some of the warehouses were already closed when I turned into Dukes Place, and the little square looked a bit forbidding in the fading daylight. It was closed in on all sides by buildings, and the synagogue on my left was fronted by tall, black railings. Nobody had lit the single street lamp that stood in the middle of the cobbles, and there was no light except for a glimmer of candles from inside the few warehouses that did not have their shutters closed. Unusually, I felt a bit nervous, realizing how private and secret the Jews were, and how separate from the rest of us. I was well used to seeing them about, black-clad and in black hats, with uncut curls of hair hanging on either side of their faces where we costers just had sideburns—but I wondered afresh whether the tales about them were true. People said there were hoards of gold and jewels in those rooms above the warehouses, and rich carpets and chandeliers and oil paintings in gold frames. The same sort of tales were told about Red Jack, but with the Jews, you could see there was a liking for fine things. Most of them were tailors or jewellers, but the poorer ones who dealt in the markets always chose odd, fancy things—feathers, quills, cigars, sponges, spectacles.

I went across to Sammy's open doorway where a few chickens scratched and pecked in the straw from the baskets of oranges, and Sammy himself looked up from the table behind the stacked display of fruit. He smiled when he saw me and said, 'Just in time, my boy. Another

15

half hour and I'd be closed.' Then he saw that I wasn't carrying a shallow, and raised his eyebrows.

Putting my request wasn't easy. 'I've been thinking,' I said. 'I mean, I'm thirteen now. I really want to be setting up on my own.'

'Thirteen,' said Sammy. 'Yes, that is the time for a boy to accept his duties.'

'Only—I don't have any money.'

'So why are you telling me?' Sammy spread his hands, but his smile was still there somewhere, and I stumbled on.

'Thing is, I don't have a shallow, because it's Curly's, and—well, I don't want to ask him any favours.'

Sammy's smile became a little more wary. 'And that's *my* problem?' he enquired. 'You costers have your own man. You should go to him.'

'Red Jack.' But I'd thought he was in too big a line of business to bother with people like me, who only wanted a shallow basket and a bit of money to buy some stock, and I frowned in confusion.

'Tell you what I'll do for you,' said Sammy. 'Just for now, I'll lend you a basket, and you can have some stock on credit. Half a crown the lot.' He reached down and produced a shallow. It was unravelling round the edges a bit, but it would do.

'Make it two bob,' I said, trying not to look too grateful. After all, business is business.

Sammy sighed. 'You'll be the death of me,' he said. 'These oranges are no rubbish, boy.' He leaned forward to pick up a cut fruit from the top of the display. 'Look at that—full of juice.'

'Two and threepence, then,' I said. 'Split the difference.'

'Done,' said Sammy rather quickly. I knew I could have got him down another penny, but he was doing me a favour.

'Drop the shallow back when you've done,' he said. 'If the shutters are down, you can leave it outside—it'll be all right. Pay me when you see me.'

We shook hands on the deal, then he stacked the shallow with oranges and gave it to me. *'Mazeltov,'* he said. *Good luck.*

3

I headed out to Islington, to try my luck round the big houses. It was more work than selling in the local market nearer home, but I didn't want to risk running into Curly—and the cooks and servants who worked in the basement kitchens were often pleased to have fruit brought to their doors. Some of them knew me now, and sometimes they'd give me old clothes or a pair of shoes. Poll was a great hand with a needle, so any garments were welcome. What couldn't be cut down for the children to wear would always sell, and there was a good trade in second-hand shoes.

It turned out to be a lucky evening. By the time I returned the shallow to Dukes Place, where the only light now came from the rooms above the warehouses, I had sold all my stock and had a good bundle of clothes—a pair of trousers that would do for Bobby and a couple of dresses with plenty of good wool cloth in them. Nice to have something to give Poll, since this might be my last night at home.

She'd miss me, I knew that. I wished my sister, Jenny, had lived. She'd have been eleven now, good company for Poll. But it was no good wishing. You have to get on with things as they are. And the next thing for me would be facing up to Curly.

Oddly enough, Curly was in quite a good mood. He was sitting in his chair by the fire when I came in, smoking his pipe and looking pleased with himself. He gave me a glance, but he didn't say anything, and neither did I. Poll had made a pot of beef stew with dumplings, and as we ate it, Curly went on about what a good price he'd got for Daisy, and how pleased he was with the new donkey and cart. He talked to Bobby mostly, which wasn't unusual. Bobby never answered back. In fact, he hardly ever answered at all, just grinned and nodded, which was the best way. Curly admired him for being such a little tough—and, of course, anyone could see that Bobby was Curly's kid. He looked just like him, with his black eyes and mop of dark hair.

I looked across at Poll and wondered why she would never tell me about my real father. Was it a man called James? I'd asked her once, but she clammed up. 'You don't want to bother about all that,' she said. 'You've got me, haven't you? What more d'you want?' And she was usually so open about things.

The meal ended and Curly went back to his seat by the fire. I still hadn't said anything about leaving home—it was a struggle to find the words, somehow. But Poll helped. She looked at me and said, 'You're very quiet tonight, Joey—what's the matter?' I guessed she knew already.

I took a deep breath. 'I want to set up on my own,' I said. 'Find somewhere else to live.'

'About time and all,' Curly cut in before Poll could say anything. 'Long as you don't come whining back to me if you make a mess of it.'

Anger flared in me again. 'Don't worry,' I said. 'You're the last person I'd ask.'

Poll looked unhappy. 'You don't have to leave home, Joey. If you're going to sell on your own, we can lend you a shallow, you could go on living here—'

'Who says?' Curly interrupted. 'Young Jess'll be

needing a shallow, and there's Ernie coming on as well. No reason why we should beggar ourselves to set His Lordship up in business.'

'I wouldn't take it anyway,' I said. 'I'll go to Red Jack.'

'You do that,' said Curly.

I stood up and grabbed my cap, heading for the door, but Curly called me back. 'Hang on,' he said, quite affably. 'No need to go blazing off like that. If you're leaving home, we may as well have a drink on it. You coming?' He knocked his pipe out against the grate and got to his feet. 'You and all, Bobby.'

'I wouldn't mind,' Bobby said. He'd always liked his beer, even since he was quite small.

I went with them, of course. If I hadn't, it would have looked as if I was sulking. I wouldn't stay long, I thought. All else apart, drinking sessions with Curly were apt to be expensive. He always ended up borrowing money, and I never got it back. Besides, I had to see Red Jack.

Following Curly and Bobby out into the street, I looked round me as if I'd become a stranger, and thought how much the place had changed since I was a nipper. There used to be a whole lot of little alleyways that connected one block of buildings to the next, and as kids we ran through them and never saw a horse or carriage. It was all different now. Great walls of brickwork had blocked off the narrow ways, and whole streets of houses had disappeared to make room for the railway. Trains went thundering by above the level of the roofs, and made the places where we lived seem smaller, somehow. At first, we'd been excited to see the smoke and sparks that billowed out from the iron monsters, but tonight I thought of all the houses that had been demolished and realized that there was less room for people like me who wanted to find a place to live.

We went up to Yellow Nell's, the other side of Aldgate High Street. The place was crowded, but there was a kind of hush because a man in the corner was reading aloud from a penny magazine. Most of the drinkers were circled round him, listening to the story, and I wanted to join them, but I stayed with Curly while he ordered the beers, and fished in my pocket for money.

'That's all right, boy,' said Curly. 'it's on me. Not every day a boy leaves home.' His voice was annoyingly loud, and I resented his playing of the proud father when both of us knew I was leaving because of our dislike of each other.

A few people glanced round at the interruption, but looked away again quickly when they saw who it was. Nobody picked a quarrel with Curly if they had any sense.

The reader raised his voice a little. 'And then the police entered, with truncheons at the ready.' Boos and whistles broke out among the listeners, and someone shouted, 'That's your peelers for you. Always there when they're not wanted.' We all hated the police. They harassed us costers the whole time, fining us half a crown if a barrow was an inch further into the road than was allowed, and if we couldn't pay on the spot, they'd impound the stock. No good pointing out that a barrow became a shop once we took up a place in the market—the police were on the side of the big shopkeepers, who didn't like us because we sold things cheaper.

Curly moved off to join a game of Three-up and Bobby went with him, so I was free to listen to the rest of the story. I looked at the magazine the man was reading from and wished I could read. Coster children didn't go to school, though—we all started working as soon as we were old enough to sell a few walnuts. The Ragged Schools were free for poor children, but we weren't free to go to them. Not that most of the coster kids wanted to. One of these days I'd learn to read, I thought. But there were other things to do first. I finished my beer and slipped out.

I went back the way we'd come, past the cab rank where the scrawny horses dozed on their feet between the shafts, heading down towards the river. I passed the Fishmongers' Hall and turned into a lane that ran between the high walls of warehouses, leading to Black Raven Alley. The mixture of smells seemed stronger at night—a yeasty reek of flour and the fragrances of tea and spices, and over it all, the wet, rotten reek of the river.

Once into the alley, I paused, not sure which of the dark doorways had Red Jack hidden behind it. A woman was standing by a lamp-post, and I asked her if she knew. 'Over there, darling,' she said. 'Third on the left. If you want a little company, I'll be here.'

I went across to the door. There didn't seem to be a knocker, so I rapped on it with my knuckles. There was no reply. I pushed at it cautiously, and it swung open, causing a bell to clang loudly above my head. Inside, it was very dark, but I heard a door open somewhere above me, and the glimmer of a candle showed a flight of worn stone steps. I wondered if I was in the right place—this seemed a dismal hole to be the home of a man as rich as Red Jack. Maybe the stories were all wrong, and he wasn't rich at all.

I climbed the stairs, turning at the half-landing, and found a woman waiting for me, staring down by the light of the candle she held. 'Who do you want?' she asked.

'Red Jack. But I'm not sure if—'

'Come in,' she said.

I stumbled up the last steps and followed her into a room that glowed with light. Two big oil lamps hung from the ceiling, and a third stood in the centre of a circular table that was covered by a red chenille cloth. A young man sat by the fire with a child on his knee, and two others were playing on the hearth-rug. The woman who had shown me in looked younger than I'd thought, now I saw her in all this warm brightness. 'I'll tell Pa,' she said, and tapped on the door of an inner room.

It was opened by a big man. He wasn't young, and I suppose he was no broader or taller than Curly, but there was a sort of assurance about him that made me feel a little afraid. He was dressed like any coster, in corduroy trousers that flared over his boots, but the waistcoat that covered his striped shirt was richly embroidered, fastened down the front with carved horn buttons, and he wore a silk neck-scarf—a kingsman, we called it—patterned with green and gold flowers. The red hair that must have given him his name had faded now to a rusty grey, but his eyes were sharp and watchful, the clear, light-brown colour of tea before you put any milk in it.

'You're Joey, aren't you,' he said. 'Sometimes known as James.'

I stood there and gawped. How did he know who I was?

Red Jack smiled, answering my unspoken question. 'There's not much I don't know, boy,' he said. 'What can I do for you?'

My thoughts had flown into confusion. 'I wanted—I mean, I haven't got any money and I need—'

'Setting up on your own?' The light-brown eyes were kind, but this was not a man with time to waste.

'Well, yes. And I need a shallow.'

He nodded. 'Sammy Meyer tells me you're a good trader,' he said. 'Shift the stock, stick to your word.' He pulled a leather-seated chair out from the table. 'Sit down, boy.' I perched myself, then sat further back when I found how comfortable the chair was, and he sat opposite me, hands clasped on the red chenille's softness. 'How much do you want?'

'Just the cost of a shallow. About ten shillings?' How strange, I thought, that he knew Sammy Meyer. Two men, so different, but both reputed to own a treasure-house. I glanced round, but there was no sign of gold or silver in the warm, homely room.

'You'll need more than that. You leaving home?'

'Yes.'

'Got anywhere to go?'

I shook my head. 'I thought I'd find a lodging-house.'

'Fourpence a night in a doss-house,' said Red Jack. 'And you'll need some stock, up front—can't have you running to Sammy all the time. I'll lend you fifteen bob, right?'

It was more money than I'd ever had. 'What's the interest rate?' I asked.

'Ten per cent. And that's half what most people charge.'

He was right. If you took a blanket down to the pawnshop, you could raise five or six pence on it, but you'd be months paying the interest. Poll had done it sometimes when Curly had lost a lot at Three-up, but as she said, it was a mug's game. So I nodded and said, 'I'll pay you back as quick as I can.'

'Right,' said Red Jack. 'Wait there.' He got up and went into the back room, then returned with a ten-bob note and a handful of coins. He counted the money out onto the red plush table cover and said, 'That do you?'

'Fine,' I said. 'Thanks very much.' We shook hands on it, then I gathered the money up and put it in my pocket. I wondered if he'd ask me to sign something—or at least, put my mark, which was the best I could do—but he didn't. 'I'll come every week and pay some back,' I promised.

'Best way,' the big man agreed. Then he got up and opened the door, and I went down the dark stairs and out into the alley. To my relief, the woman who had stood by the lamp-post was no longer there.

4

The next morning, I bought myself a good shallow from the basket-maker in Brick Lane, then went up to Sammy's for some stock. I had my spare clothes with me, tied in a bundle, because tonight I wouldn't be going home. The thought of the unknown adventure that lay ahead made my stomach churn a little, but I tried to ignore it.

'Good boy,' said Sammy when he saw the new shallow. 'That's the way. Down on your luck one day and a businessman the next. You'll go far.'

'Don't know about far,' I said. 'But I've got to go somewhere.' Curly had come back from the pub in one of his worst moods last night, having lost all his money and even his neck-scarf at Three-up. He'd get laughed at in the market today—everyone knew what a coster had been up to if he was out in the streets without his kingsman. It was a mark of shame and ridicule. Well, serve him right.

'You want to leave your bundle here?' asked Sammy. 'Fetch it when you've found yourself a place.'

'Thanks,' I said. 'That would be good.' I paid him for my stock of oranges and set off.

It was one of my best days, and I was back to Sammy twice for more supplies. Then, as the daylight faded and the lamps were being lit, I came back along Middlesex Street with my empty shallow slung by its strap across my shoulder. I'd leave the bundle where it was.

The market was in its usual crowded confusion, with stalls on both sides of the narrow street still doing good business and hawkers offering you everything you could want. Bootlaces, corn plasters, mousetraps, nutmeg graters, blotting paper—there were a thousand useful things as well as flowers and ribbons and all the pretty stuff that girls like. The beggars were out in force, too, some of them with a missing arm or leg—though Blind Ned could see as well as anyone else when he chose. He just had the trick of turning his eyes up under his open lids so that only the whites showed.

The smells made my mouth water. Fried fish, meat pies, stewed eels, and hot green peas, and the cake stalls with their spicy Chelsea buns and their gingerbread, hot toffee—no end to it. I bought a hunk of plum duff and ate it as I walked. Some people pushed their way through the crowd as if they were in a hurry to get somewhere, but most of them were like me, happy to drift along and look at it all.

Above the noise of feet on cobbles and costers shouting their wares—or beating drums if their voices had given out like Curly's had—I heard a girl singing from somewhere further along the street. It was Rose, I thought, recognizing her clear voice. Rose had been having a hard time lately. Her mother had died last spring of the cough that had made her so gaunt and hollow. Consumption, they called it—a good name for a disease that devoured people from within. So Rose was on her own, looking after her brother and sister. Singing was easier than selling violets, she said—it left her hands free so she could grab Stevie if she had to. He was one of those little boys who are into everything.

I made my way down the street towards her, licking my fingers that were sticky from the plum duff. I could see a top-hatted man on a horse trying to push his way

27

through the crowd, and thought vaguely that he was going a bit fast—then there was a commotion, and Rose's song broke off in a scream.

Careless of who I barged into, I ran to see what had happened. The crowd round the Punch and Judy show were intent as the story came to its end, but I pushed through. Rose's scream was still ringing in my ears, and I was sure something awful was going on.

A lot of people were gathered round the horse and its rider. I knew who he was—Mr Meachum, who came to collect rent for the landlords. None of us liked him. He used to come on foot when I was a kid, and he had chilblains on his fingers, but he'd risen in the world since then. I stared at him in horror as he beat at the people round him with his riding whip, a fat man now, with double chins that bulged over his white cravat and pale kid gloves on his hands. A couple of costers were holding the horse's bridle, ducking from the blows he aimed at them—and then I saw Rose, bent double as she came from under the animal, clutching Stevie in her arms. The frightened horse was trampling uneasily, and I saw that the little boy Rose held had blood trickling down his face from where he had been kicked or trodden on. I thought for a terrible moment that he was dead, he looked so limp and white—but then he gave a little choking sound and began to cry.

Still holding her little brother, Rose turned to face the rider. 'You could have killed him!' she shouted. 'You got no right to ride through here that fast!'

Meachum tightened his mouth in a sneer and cut at her with his whip. Rose ducked, and I was near enough to fling up an arm and catch the blow. 'I'll ride where I like,' he said. 'You think I'll keep Lord Rivers waiting because you can't keep your snivelling brat under control? Get out of my way.' He whacked the grey horse across its hindquarters, jerking its head to and fro to break the grip of the hands that held reins and bridle, then drove it savagely forward. There were yells of protest as people leapt out of the way, but nobody tried to stop him. Meachum was well known to be in with the police, and there was no point in asking for trouble.

Rose dabbed at Stevie's face with the corner of her shawl. Her little sister, Meg, was clutching at her skirts and wailing with alarm, and even though I was grown-up now, I wished Poll was here, because she'd have known what to do. 'We need some water,' I said, looking at the swollen wound on the little boy's head.

'He'll be all right,' Rose said. 'Won't you, Stevie?' She bent her head to kiss the little boy in her arms, soothing his sobs, and I suddenly thought she was like a little hen turning the eggs under her warm feathers, and felt all melted inside. I gave a sort of cough, embarrassed at feeling so mushy. I wanted to do something practical— but what?

A man's voice from behind me said, 'You'd best let my wife have a look at that.'

Pocky Dan was gazing down at us, and his pitted face was full of concern. He wore no jacket, having come straight from the Punch and Judy booth, and his shirt sleeves were rolled up in spite of the cold. His straw-coloured hair looked sweaty from working in the hot little space behind the stage, and the girl of about eight who stood beside him in a grubby spangled dress looked hot, too. Their brown-patched terrier had come with them, still wearing its ruff, and it sat up on its hind legs and whined in comic concern.

'Poor little kid,' said the girl, staring at Stevie. 'What happened?'

'He got run over by Meachum,' said her father. 'Looks as if a hoof caught him. Kate, what do you think?'

Pocky's wife had come to join him, a dimpled woman with curly brown hair. She wore a striped red skirt, and the younger children who had come with her were in bits and pieces of spangled costume from their jobs as dancers and tambourine-shakers before the show.

'Goose-grease,' Kate said firmly. 'Come on back to the booth, I've got some there. Never know when you'll want it with children.' She looked again and added, 'You're Rose, aren't you? I've heard you singing.'

Rose nodded. Her face was white now, and I noticed for the first time that she had freckles on her nose. Everyone started to move off to the Punch and Judy booth and I went, too, though it was nothing to do with me, really.

'I was sorry to hear about your mother,' Kate said to Rose.

'Yes.' What else could she say? Nothing could be changed—you just had to get on with it.

There was a pause, then as we came to the booth, deserted by its audience now, Kate added, 'We're always here if you need any help, Rose. Just give us a shout.'

'I will,' said Rose. 'Thank you.' And I wished I was the one who had offered help, because I suddenly knew that I wanted to be with Rose all the time, and take care of her. But I had no place to live, and nothing to give her. I turned and walked away.

5

It seemed odd, walking through the streets and not knowing where I'd spend the night. I wanted very much to head back to Grigg's Court and the crowded room that smelt so comfortably of our family, but I couldn't go creeping back there, not after what Curly had said last night. *Sooner you're out of here the better—you've been on my back long enough.*

No point in thinking about it. I was grown-up now, I didn't need Poll's pot of soup on the stove or the line of washing that hung above the fire or the warmth of the blanket I shared with Bobby at night. I was thirteen, nearly fourteen, old enough to be on my own. Scarborough Street was the place for lodging-houses, I'd heard. It wasn't far away, just over towards Whitechapel.

Rose kept coming back into my mind as I walked. For a skinny little thing, she was so brave, standing up to Meachum like that. A proper little fighting sparrow. One day, perhaps, I'd ask her to move in with me. Plenty of boys my age had found themselves a girl, and I could see why. All questions of liking apart, it took two of you to earn enough money for a room of your own, specially now there was such a shortage of places. With so many houses knocked down for the railway, the ones left were jammed with people, and the landlords kept putting the rents up, because nobody could refuse to pay.

I wondered how anyone came to be a landlord and make all that money. Some men were born rich, of course, like the Lord Rivers that Meachum had mentioned. *You think I'll keep Lord Rivers waiting?* Perhaps he was even richer than Red Jack, who could lend me fifteen shillings as if it was twopence. One day, perhaps, I'd get a bit of money together, and find a room for Rose and me.

Scarborough Street had terraced houses along both sides of it, and the place stank. It was no more than a muddy lane, and as I trod my way through the refuse that had been thrown out to rot, I was hit by the stench of human filth that came from the houses with their open front doors. I almost turned back, thinking to spend the night in some square where there were benches under the trees, but it was too cold for that—and who did I think I was, anyway? These doss-houses existed for people like me, who had nowhere else to go. I went in through the nearest door and joined the people who were standing in the narrow hall.

A candle glimmered from a small table where a man sat, taking money from the waiting people and writing their names in a big book. He had thin hair combed across a balding head, and when he looked up, I saw that he was hollow-cheeked as if he had few teeth left, although he was not old—not that it was unusual. Most of us had trouble with our teeth. I'd seen the man before, standing in the market with a tray round his neck that held paper and envelopes, quill pens, and a carefully wedged bottle of ink. Quill Quennell, they called him, the screever—a man who would write a letter for anyone who asked, provided they had a penny. He was good at begging-letters, people said, and that was his main use, writing appealing sob-stories that sometimes won a few shillings from a rich man.

A bare-footed Irishwoman was in front of me, and when she had given her name and paid her two pence, Quennell looked up at me.

'Name?'

I don't know what came over me in that instant, but somehow, I wanted to keep my real name out of that stinking place. My nickname, which I didn't like much, would do.

'James,' I said.

'James what?'

Again I hesitated. Curly's name was Barker, but that was nothing to do with me. 'Rivers,' I said wildly, as Meachum's voice rang again in my mind.

Quennell wrote it down and looked at it, and when he met my eyes again he was frowning in perplexity. 'Where did you get that name?' he asked.

'No crime in it, is there?' I tried to sound tough, but I was scared—maybe you weren't allowed to pinch another man's name, specially if he was a lord.

'No crime at all,' said Quennell. 'It's just—unusual. For a coster boy, I mean.' He smiled and added, 'No offence.' He still had his two front teeth among the decayed stumps of the others, and this, together with his slightly bulging dark eyes, made him look like a rabbit.

James Rivers, I thought, quite pleased now to have given myself such a grand name in this filthy place. *No offence*. Quennell had sounded almost respectful. I could be who I liked, it was no crime. I dropped my two pence into the box on the table and walked on into the evil-smelling house. Then I paused. Was there some expected order in letting out the beds? Where should I go? I turned back to ask, but Quennell was wrangling with the weedy-looking man who had been standing behind me.

'I've only got three halfpence,' the man was whining. 'Come on, Mr Quennell, let me in. I'll pay you the other halfpenny tomorrow, honest.'

Quennell shook his head. 'I've told you before, Johnny Pink,' he said. 'No credit. I don't make the rules, I only work here.'

The man called Johnny Pink sniffed and wiped his nose on the back of his hand. 'I'll sleep on the kitchen floor, then,' he said. 'That's one thing about the old clothes trade—you can always make yourself comfortable.' He grinned, pointing to the large, frowsty-smelling pack he carried, and I was glad once again that I was a coster, dealing in fruit and vegetables. The only time they got smelly was if something had gone bad, and you could easily sort that out.

'One penny, then,' Quennell said to Johnny Pink. 'And don't let me catch you in any of the rooms. I don't want to get into trouble.' He wrote Pink's name down. 'Next?'

Johnny Pink shuffled his way along the dark passage, limping a bit under the weight of the big pack. I followed him, and asked where I should go.

'Anywhere you like,' he said. 'Pick any bed that's not taken. If you're hungry, there's grub in the kitchen. It's down here.'

He headed off down a flight of narrow wooden stairs, and I went as well. It led to a basement room with a low ceiling, so thick with smoke that I could hardly see across it. A brazier burned under an iron chimney, and although the reek of it made my eyes run, there was also a good smell of boiling saveloy sausages from the big pot that stood there. A woman was dealing them out with hunks of bread, and I went over and asked for one.

'That'll be a halfpenny,' she said. 'You got the money?'

'Yes.' I paid her, and she nodded.

'Mustard?'

'Yes, please.'

I found a space between two men on one of the benches by the wall, and sat down to eat. The bread was thick and fresh, and the spicy, red-skinned sausage warmed my stomach and made me feel better. I looked round me, noticing that the floor was of trodden earth and that rough wooden posts held up the low beams of the ceiling. A lot of people were clustered round the beer barrels that stood on trestles near the brazier, and Johnny Pink was among them. He spotted me and came across with a mug of ale in his hand to squeeze in beside me.

'Couldn't lend me twopence, could you?' he asked. 'Now I've bought this, I'm skint.' He took a draught of his ale and wiped his mouth on his sleeve, then added, 'Pay you back tomorrow, honest.'

I shook my head. There was money in my pocket, but it wouldn't last long if I started dishing it out to people like Pink, who quite obviously wouldn't pay it back tomorrow or any day. Red Jack's loan had to be repaid, and I needed to save every farthing if I was to escape from places like this.

The scrawny man looked at me suspiciously. 'You a nark?' he asked.

''Course not.' A nark was someone who ran with tales to the police. 'What d'you mean?' I was indignant. 'Costers don't have any truck with the peelers.'

'No, a house nark,' said Pink. 'There's always one. A bloke who gets a free night's lodging as long as he makes a note of who's here. It's to check up on old Quennell, see. Make sure he don't let anyone in free.'

'Who does the house belong to, then?'

'Dunno,' said Pink. 'Some lord what owns the whole street, I wouldn't wonder. Doesn't matter, does it? All the same to us.'

I was thinking about the rabbit-faced man. 'I wouldn't like to be Quennell, working for someone else.'

'He's all right,' said Pink. 'Better off than most, being able to read and write. But he's got expensive tastes, has Quennell. Spends his money quicker than he can earn it.

Be seeing you.' He got up and moved off towards a man standing by one of the wooden posts, and I heard him repeat his request for a loan.

I left the kitchen and climbed the stairs, still carrying my empty shallow and feeling glad I'd left my bundle of spare clothes with Sammy. A night or two in the same togs wouldn't do any harm, and I could see this was the sort of place where stuff would get stolen the minute you took your eye off it.

I looked into one room after another. They were all the same, dim and smelly, with narrow beds packed close together, and every bed seemed to have someone sitting or lying on it. I went up another staircase to the top of the house, where a door stood open under the sloping attic roof. There were six beds in this small room. Three were occupied, and a couple lay kissing on a fourth, but two were empty, so I put my shallow down on one of them. A reeking bucket stood in the middle of the floor for use as a toilet, so full that I could see nobody had emptied it for days. We used a chamber pot at home, to save going down to the outside privy in the middle of the night, but Poll emptied and washed it every morning.

There must be a privy here, I thought. I'd have to go down to the yard and find it. But I didn't want someone else to take my bed, and I didn't want anyone to pinch my shallow. Two little boys lay together in the bed next to mine. The younger one was asleep, but his older brother, who looked about six, was watching me. I bent down and whispered, 'Watch my basket for me? I'll be back in a minute. I'll give you a farthing,' I added.

'Cor, thanks,' he said, and propped himself on his elbow, awake and responsible.

On my way back from the yard outside the basement kitchen, I came up into the narrow hall and saw two men at the little table with its lighted candle. One was

Quennell, lean and stooping, his fingers pressed nervously on the table's wooden surface while the other ran an eye over the names written in the ledger. This was a solidly-built man in a frock coat and top hat, a white cravat gleaming at his neck in the candlelight, and as he turned to put the book back in its place, I saw who he was. Meachum. He snapped shut the steel clasp of a heavy leather bag, and picked it up. Then, without so much as a nod of farewell to the meek man who stood behind the table, he opened the front door with his pale-gloved hand, and went out into the night.

6

When I woke the next morning, my arms and legs were covered with bites. I'd slept in my clothes under the thin blanket, and I sat up, scratching at my itching ankles, then pushed my feet into my boots. The sky outside the small attic window was still dark, but I wanted to be out of the stinking, bug-infested house. I put my cap on, picked up my shallow and groped my way down the stairs.

It was the beginning of a bad time. For the rest of that week I sold oranges and slept in doss-houses, trying several different ones. Some were even worse than the one where Quennell worked—at least you could get food there. On Saturday evening I went to Black Raven Alley to pay back a first instalment on my set-up money, and Red Jack looked at me and said, 'How are you doing, boy?'

'Not bad,' I said. 'Making a bit.'

'That's the stuff.' But the fox-brown eyes had not shifted from my face. 'Missing home, are you?'

'Kind of.' I couldn't have said any more, because a wave of wanting to be back in Grigg's Court had washed over me. I thought of silly things, like the patch of brown paper Poll had stuck over a broken window and the barrel of apples in the corner that Curly had bought cheap. There was no smell of sweet apples in the doss-houses.

'It's always bad at the start,' Red Jack said. 'I've been there, I know.'

'Go on?' Surprise made me forget my complaints.

The big man laughed. 'You think I was born into money? I never had any more than you when I was a nipper. Just keep your pecker up, right? See you next week.'

A cold wind was blowing as I walked towards Whitechapel for another night in a lodging-house, and despite Red Jack's advice, I felt utterly alone. Even Lucky Luke had the company of whatever dog he'd stolen, I thought. But it wasn't a dog I wanted, it was the company of a proper family. I missed Bobby and Poll and the little ones, Jess and Ernie—the sound of their voices, the feel of a small, grubby hand in mine. I envied Rose her closeness with Meg and Stevie, and wondered if the little boy had recovered from the cut on his head. I'd looked for Rose every day as I went round the streets, selling, but there had been no sign of her.

The next morning was a Sunday. The streets were empty and quiet when I came out of the doss-house, bitten and itching as usual. Most of the costers took a day off on Sunday and treated themselves to a roast joint for dinner if they could afford it—but a day of idleness was no use to me. Where would I spend it?

The Jewish warehouses would be open, as Sunday wasn't their Sabbath, so I went up to Dukes Place for stock. I wondered whether to go down to Middlesex Street—Petticoat Lane, some called it—where the morning market would be in full swing, but decided to stick with the big houses in Finsbury.

It had been raining, and thick mud mingled with the horse-dung in the streets, but people were about now, well-dressed ladies and gentlemen with leather-covered books under their arms, answering the call of the church bells. I supposed the books they carried must be Bibles or hymn books. The City Missionaries came and read Bible stories to us sometimes, down in the markets, then they went on about Jesus and how we had to be good. We didn't take a lot of notice. They were all right, though, the missionaries. Sometimes they'd buy a whole shilling's worth of oranges and give them away to the kids, and that was good business.

At Bloomfield Street I stopped to let a carriage go by— very smart, drawn by a pair of high-stepping bays—and a couple of boys and a girl got busy as soon as the road was clear, sweeping a crossing so the ladies and gentlemen wouldn't get their skirts and trousers muddied. And I saw that the girl was Rose.

My heart seemed to jump with happiness. I watched her as she swept her way towards me, the wind blowing her red hair, then she saw me and smiled over her shoulder, turning to hold a hand out to the people who crossed. 'Spare a farthing, sir!' she begged them. 'Kind lady, spare a farthing!' One of the boys got a coin, but she got nothing. She came to join me.

'Why aren't you singing?' I asked. 'That's a better trade, isn't it?'

Rose shrugged. 'No good on a Sunday. I was singing outside St Martin's one Sunday a couple of weeks back, thinking I'd make a bit when they came out of church, and a woman gave me a right telling-off. Said it was disrespectful, singing on the Lord's Day. But they'd been singing inside, with the organ playing, I'd heard them. And what about the birds? I nearly said to her, if the Lord don't like it, why does he let the sparrows chirp and the pigeons coo?'

I laughed, then asked, 'What about Stevie? Is he all right?'

'Oh, yes. He was poorly for a day or two, woke up at night with headaches, but he's all right now. I left him and Meg at home, locked them in for safety. They can't help on the crossings, and I'm scared they might get run over. I'll take them some bread at dinner time—with any luck.'

One of the sweeper-boys said, 'Thank you, sir,' and put a coin in his pocket, and Rose made a face. 'They get more than I do. But it's their crossing by rights, so I can't expect to make as much.'

A passing cob, ridden by a man in a brown frock-coat, lifted its docked tail and left a trail of droppings, and the two boys were out at once, brushing the muck aside.

'Missed that one, didn't I,' said Rose.

I took three oranges from my shallow—good, big ones—and held them out to her. 'One each,' I said. 'You and Meg and Stevie.'

'But I can't—'

'I don't want any money for them. Go on—take them.'

I piled the oranges into her hands, and she looked down at them for a moment. Then she lifted her face to mine and kissed me.

The delight of it made my face turn red. She blushed as well, and we stood there and stared at each other, half-laughing, as if we couldn't believe what had happened.

All the rest of that day, I felt warm and happy each time I thought of Rose's kiss—which was often. And I sold well, of course—selling is always easier when you're happy, because people like being smiled at. A housekeeper in a pleated white cap gave me some children's clothes wrapped in newspaper. She even tied them up with string. 'The young master and mistress have got new outfits,' she said, 'and I dare say you have little brothers and sisters. It's all been washed,' she added. 'Tell your mother there's no need to do that.'

I thanked her, not getting too close in case she noticed that I was pretty unwashed myself. Sleeping in the doss-houses, the best I could do was a quick sluice under the pump in the yard, and I hadn't thought what to do about clothes. Poll used to take all our stuff down to the public wash-house once a week, but my spare clothes were still at Sammy's, waiting for—what? *Mazeltov.* A change of luck, perhaps.

Looking back on it now, I suppose I changed my own luck, that day when I walked round Finsbury and thought about Rose. It was costing me twopence a night to sleep in the doss-houses, but wouldn't it be better to give the money to Rose, if she would find me a corner somewhere to sleep in? I could help to buy food for her and the little ones, and I was used to young children—I could give her a hand, looking after them. These were excuses, of course. What I really wanted was to be with Rose all the time, to take her in my arms and kiss her freckled face. I wouldn't be like Curly, I'd take proper care of her and be kind. But wasn't it a cheek to think she'd take me in when I had so little to offer? I'd always thought I'd wait until I had some money behind me.

In the late afternoon, I bought a big white loaf in the market, and some ham, and four steaming hot gingerbread cakes. Then I walked down past the cab rank as if I was going back to Grigg's Court, but went on past there to the next block of buildings, Sugarloaf Court. Some of it had been knocked down because the railway passed close overhead on its high arches, and I didn't know which part of it Rose lived in. I looked up at the grimy windows, many of them broken, and a passing woman glanced at me suspiciously.

42

I asked, 'Do you know where Rose lives?'

She didn't smile. 'Rose who?'

'Um—I think it's Chappell.' I'd never thought to ask her surname, but I seemed to remember it from somewhere. 'Red Rose, they call her.'

The woman gave me an even colder look, and I suddenly knew what she was thinking. *Her not fourteen yet, and she's on the game already*. But she shrugged as if it was none of her business, and said, 'Over there. End door, second floor. The room at the back.'

'Thanks. I'm just a friend,' I called after her, but the woman didn't look back.

I climbed the stairs and knocked on the door with my knuckles. Meg opened it. She beamed up at me and said over her shoulder, 'It's the orange man.'

'Who?' Rose came to look, and I was full of fear that she'd say I couldn't come in. This was her home, I couldn't expect to be part of it. But her eyes lit up when she saw me, and her lips parted in a little gasp. 'Joey!'

'I just brought these,' I blurted, and pushed the bread and the ham and the gingerbread into her arms, half turning away to forestall disappointment.

'Oh, Joey.' Her hand was on my arm. 'Don't go.'

And without quite knowing how, I was in the room with her and the children, and the rest of the world was outside.

We sat by the small fire for a long time after Meg and Stevie had been tucked into the bed they shared, but as it grew later, we ran out of things to say, and an awkward silence grew. We'd talked about everything except the question that hung unasked between us, and it was Rose who said bravely, 'What are you going to do? Are you going back to the doss-house?'

I felt my face colour. 'Could I stay here for the night? I'll be fine down here by the fire.' There was a rug, hand-made from woven strips of rag.

'All right,' said Rose.

I said, 'I'll just—nip out the back.'

'All right,' she said again.

When I got back from the yard, she was curled up in the wall bed, and there was a folded blanket on the rag rug in front of the dying fire. I took off my jacket and my boots and pulled the blanket over me, then blew the candle out. I wondered whether to say goodnight, but didn't want to wake her if she was already asleep.

I dreamed that I was very small, wandering in strange streets. A dog came up to me, and because I was so small, its face was on a level with mine. *Poor dog*, I thought. *You're lost, too.* Lucky Luke must have stolen it from its owners, and now he, too, had lost it. The dog's fur was gently brushing my face. *Are you cold?* it asked.

'Joey, are you cold?'

It wasn't a dog. Rose was crouching beside me. Her hair was in my face and her hand on my shoulder. 'What is it?' she whispered. 'What's the matter?'

I propped myself on my elbow, and found I was shivering. The fire was dead, and a cold moon shone through the cracked window.

'You were moaning,' said Rose. 'I thought you were ill.'

'No. Just dreaming.'

'What about?'

'I was lost.' And I leaned my face against the soft hollow of her neck as if I was a child again, protected and safe.

'You're freezing,' said Rose. 'Come on.' She got to her

feet and took my hand, pulling me up, and I stumbled after her to the wall bed. The disapproving face of the woman outside came into my mind, and I started to say, 'I didn't mean—'

Rose hushed me, pulling the blanket over us both. 'I know you didn't,' she said. 'It's all right. Go to sleep.' And as gratefully as a homeless dog brought in from the cold, I slept.

7

I collected my bundle from Sammy the next day, when I'd finished selling. 'Thanks for keeping it so long,' I said, and fished in my pocket for a coin to give him.

'Keep your money, my boy,' said Sammy. 'I don't charge for a kindness. May you be happy.'

Oh, and I was happy. In the months that followed, I paid off my debt to Red Jack, and with Rose and me both working, it wasn't too hard to find the money for the rent. Little Meg grew into quite a good singer as well, learning all the words and piping up with Rose in the streets and markets, and at four, Stevie took himself seriously as a seller of almonds and walnuts, though I always relieved him of his little tray of stock if he seemed to be getting tired.

Sometimes Rose and I treated ourselves to an evening out. Betsy Green who lived across the landing said she'd listen out in case the little ones wanted anything, so we were free to have a bit of fun. We went to the Coburg Theatre once or twice, which everyone called 'The Vic', but I liked the penny gaffs better. They were just makeshift places where a theatre had been set up in an empty shop. The stage was at the back, and there was a rough gallery built above the shop entrance, to give the audience a good view. There was a smashing one near Smithfield—you could hear the music from streets away, and it had big posters outside under a blaze of gaslight, with pictures of the singers and artistes, dressed in ostrich feathers and not much else. Betsy Green said you wouldn't catch her spending good money to look at some hussy's legs, but we just laughed. Betsy's man had gone off with an actress years ago, so you could see how she felt.

One Saturday night, we were all packed into the gallery at the Smithfield gaff, roaring out the choruses and eating jellied eels with vinegar on them and having a great time, when trouble broke out. Some of the men in the audience were drunker than usual, and a couple of them started joining in with the verses of the songs, which just wasn't done. The singer on the stage does the verse, then the crowd joins in for the chorus. So when these drunks started bawling along with the verses, people shouted at them to shut up, and there was a bit of a scuffle. When the song ended, the woman who ran the place came onto the stage and yelled, 'No fighting in the gallery, or you're out!' She had yellow hair and strong arms, and her henchmen cuffed a few heads just to get the message across.

Another singer came on, but the rumpus in the gallery didn't stop. 'I can sing as good as that old tart down there!' a man bawled—and I realized with a lurch of dread that it was Curly.

'Throw him out!' people were shouting, but Curly and his drunken mates shouted back, and when one of the bouncers tried to grab Curly, he got a punch on the nose that sent him reeling back into the woman who was selling pigs' trotters. Her tray went flying and so did the trotters. One of them hit a girl in the eye, and the man she was with stood up and took a swing at the bloke he thought had thrown it, only he hadn't, and in the next minute the place was in uproar. Curly and his mates were in the thick of it, and the bouncers grabbed the heavy sticks they kept for emergencies and waded in, not bothering much who

47

they whacked. A hurled beer mug just missed the singer on the stage, who was trying to keep going, so she shrugged and walked off, and so did the pianist and the drummer and the man who played the violin, and the curtain came down.

I stayed where I was, hoping Curly wouldn't spot me and drag me into it, but the bouncers were shoving people down the stairs and the yellow-haired woman was bawling, 'All out, the lot of you!' And we hadn't even got to the interval. Trust Curly to muck things up.

'It's not your fault,' Rose said as we walked home, earlier than we'd expected. 'You don't have to look so miserable.'

'I just hate the thought that he's anything to do with me,' I said.

'But he isn't,' Rose pointed out. 'You told me yourself, he's not your father. You don't even look like him.'

I said, 'I wish I knew who my real father was. I can't see why Poll wouldn't tell me.'

'And I can't see why you want to know,' said Rose. 'What difference does it make?'

'It could have made a lot of difference if he really was some sort of toff like people say.'

'I wouldn't take too much notice of that,' Rose said. 'Could have just been a joke because you sounded a bit prissy when you were small. You still do sometimes, when you get on your high horse.'

'Well, thanks,' I said huffily. 'Fat lot of help you are.'

Rose's arm through mine hugged a little closer. 'I wouldn't want to change you, silly. You're all right as you are. Why do you want things different?'

'I don't want them different. I just want to know.'

'Honest,' said Rose with a sigh, 'sometimes I wonder why I love you.'

She'd never said she loved me before, not in words.

She reached up to kiss me untidily as we walked, so I had to stop and let her do it again properly, and by the time we'd sorted all that out, my bad temper was forgotten.

In the room where Meg and Stevie slept peacefully, Rose knelt down to coax the fire back into life, feeding it with small sticks and blowing at it. When a flame started up, she sat back on her heels and looked at me.

'You know what?' she said. 'I reckon you ought to learn to read. You're not like me, just getting on with what has to be done, you're always asking questions and fretting about ideas. You'd like reading. My ma could read. She started teaching me, but she died before I'd really got the hang of it. She used to say it's like listening to voices.'

'I've always wanted to read,' I said.

'Well, then. Why don't you ask Quill Quennell? You know him. He's in the market every day, with his tray of paper and stuff. And I don't reckon he'd charge much. If he does, we'll just have to save up.'

She made it sound so simple.

I walked past Quennell a couple of times the next day. The first time, he was writing something at the dictation of a distraught-looking woman who clutched a baby in a shawl, and the second time, I was just shaping up to ask him when Lucky Luke came by and thumped me cheerfully on the shoulder. He had no dog with him, but he was wearing a pair of new, shiny boots.

'You're doing well,' I said.

Lucky grinned. 'You can say that again. I made four pounds last week, on a poodle. The owners were going mad, wanting it back.'

'Four *pounds*?' I couldn't believe it. Quennell had moved away, but I'd have to catch him later.

'That's nothing,' Lucky said. 'Up west, there's finders making hundreds of pounds. Hundreds. You'd be amazed what the toffs will pay to get their pooches back. They have the pedigree sort, see. Worth a lot.'

'How do you go about it, then?'

'I work with George Bolsover, the dog-meat man. He knows all the houses where there's dogs, gives me the tip-off. I nick the mutt, first chance I get, and after a couple of days George writes a notice saying it's been found, sticks it on a lamp-post near the house. (He can write, George, he's a proper businessman.) Apply to the King's Arms.'

'Then you meet them and give the dog back, get the reward?'

'That's the idea. Got to be careful, though, the toffs are starting to cut up rough about it.'

'Well, they would, wouldn't they.' I glanced round. 'You don't know where Quill Quennell lives, do you? I wanted a word with him.'

'Over the baker's shop in Middlesex Street,' Lucky said promptly, then added, 'Has he got any money?'

'Don't think so.' Nobody would work in that doss-house if they could afford not to.

'Pity. He might have been worth a touch—he's got a dog.'

'You leave him alone,' I said, suddenly protective of the rabbit-faced man, and Lucky grinned.

'Keep your hair on, James. See you.' And he went off through the crowd, treading a little gingerly, as if his feet weren't used to the new boots yet.

I went to see Quennell the next morning, after I'd sold my first lot of fruit. I was doing apples mostly, as it was

autumn now, and the oranges wouldn't start for another
week or two. His room was in the attic, up four flights of
narrow stairs from the door beside the baker's shop, and it
took him some time to answer my tap at his door. When
he did, he was wearing a dressing gown over a rumpled
shirt and trousers, and I could see he'd only just got up.

'Mr Rivers,' he said, and gave me his sweet, ruined
smile. 'Do come in.'

The room was very small, with a leather-topped desk
standing by the casement window between sloping rafters,
and the shelves on the wall held more books than I'd ever
seen, twenty or thirty of them. A thin, fawn-coloured dog
looked up from where it lay on the unmade bed, trembling
a little, and Quennell stroked it. 'No need to be nervous,
Sadie, James is a friend.' Then he glanced back at me and
added, 'Do sit down.'

There was a chair on either side of the desk, so I
perched on the nearest one and he sat opposite me,
running his fingers through the strands of his dark hair in
an attempt to tidy it. 'What can I do for you?'

'I wondered if you'd teach me to read,' I said. 'And
what it would cost.' Rose and I had worked out that we
could go to seven pence a week if necessary.

He looked at me thoughtfully, and I glanced away,
faintly embarrassed. Would he think it a cheek that a
common coster-boy wanted to join this world of books and
ink and fine, white paper? A decanter of ruby-red liquid
stood on the desk with a smeared glass beside it, and I
wondered absently what it was. I'd never seen wine so
clear and bright.

Quennell picked the flask and glass up and put them
away in a small cupboard, then sat down again. 'Have you
always wanted to read?' he asked.

I couldn't see that it was any of his business. He caught
my slight frown and was apologetic at once. 'Forgive me,

I was just curious. Yes, of course I will teach you.' Then he asked, 'Where do you live, James?'

'Sugarloaf Court.'

'And where is that?'

'Just off the Minories, by the railway.'

'Have you always lived there?'

'About a year. I was in Grigg's Court before.'

'With—your parents?'

I boiled over. 'What's that got to do with it?'

'Nothing, nothing. Just a silly idea of mine.' He took a sheet of paper from the desk drawer and picked a pencil from an old jug that held a clutter of quills. 'Now—let's make a start. First, I'll show you how to write your name. There are five letters in James and six in Rivers.'

I didn't correct him about my name, though I might have done if he hadn't asked so many questions.

8

An hour later, I went down the narrow stairs to the street with my mind full of the shapes and sounds of letters—and almost collided with Pocky Dan, who was trundling past with the folded-up Punch and Judy booth on its barrow. One of his youngest children was riding on the top, and the others were walking beside him.

'Hallo, Joe,' he said when he saw me. 'How's things?' He always called me Joe. Rose had got to know his family well since Stevie's accident, and sang for them sometimes as a warm-up to the show—but he wouldn't call me Joey. That was the showman's name for a clown, he said, and I was no clown, was I?

He stopped the barrow, and I told him about Quennell and the reading. I was feeling pretty pleased about it, because the rabbit-faced man had said he'd only charge me a penny a time, which was a lot less than I'd expected.

'That's good,' said Pocky—but his scarred face looked concerned, and he went on, 'Just be careful about Quennell, though. You know he's in with Meachum.'

'He only takes money for him in the doss-house,' I protested. 'He's not friends with him or anything.'

Pocky looked at me. Then he fished a few coins from his pocket and said to the eldest of the children, 'Sarah, take the little 'uns into the baker's, get them a bun apiece.'

They rushed off, and Pocky turned back to me. 'Listen,

Joe, there's things you don't understand. Quennell takes opium. And people who do that—well, you have to be a bit careful of them.'

I frowned, thinking of the decanter that Quennell had quietly removed from the desk. 'Is opium red stuff, like cherry syrup?'

Pocky nodded. 'That's the liquid form of it. Laudanum, they call it.'

'I've heard of that,' I said. 'It's just I'd never seen it.' I couldn't see what the fuss was about. 'People buy it from the chemist. Poll knew a woman who used to put a few drops of it in her baby's bottle—said it stopped him crying.'

'It would do that all right,' said Pocky. 'Cures all pains and calms all worries, they say. I reckon Quennell started using it because of his teeth. There's no pain worse than bad toothache, and he's had a lot of that. But the thing is, Joe, once you're hooked, you can't do without it. And the stuff's expensive.'

Got expensive tastes, has Quennell. Johnny Pink's words in the doss-house came back to me, and I nodded with new understanding. So that was why Quennell looked so shabby and thin. If it came to a choice between laudanum and food, the red liquid won every time.

'It's made from poppies in China,' Pocky said. 'Comes in through the docks as resin—looks a bit like putty. And the thing is, if you're in the know, you can get it a lot cheaper.' He asked my question for me. 'Who's in the know? Well, the shipping magnates, for a start. They import the stuff. But they use agents to do things for them—people like Meachum—and the Meachums are in a position to hand out favours. They can supply cheap opium, and they do. But they ask their favours in return. That's why Quennell works at the doss-house, Joe. He can't refuse.'

It was horribly clear.

'There's a lot of nasty jobs get done by people like poor Quennell,' Pocky went on. 'People who owe a favour and can't say no. So there's spying and tale-telling and theft and sudden death in the middle of the night, and nobody will say what they know. It's dirty work on a big scale, done by little people.'

'What's dirty work?' one of the children chirped up. They'd come out of the shop, happily biting into currant buns.

'Anything that gets your hands mucky,' Pocky told him. 'Know what I mean, Joe?'

I nodded gloomily. I'd rather not have known. Somehow I liked Quennell. There was a sweetness about him that had seemed trustworthy. *Shows how wrong you can be*, I thought.

'Don't look so down,' Pocky said. 'It's great that he's teaching you to read. But just remember, he's Meachum's man. And whatever you do, keep away from the red stuff.'

'What red stuff?' asked the same child.

'Cherry syrup. Too much gives you collywobbles. Wipe your hands, Danny.' He produced a grubby handkerchief and rubbed the stickiness from the little boy's fingers, then picked up the barrow's shafts. 'See you, Joe.' And he went off up the street, whistling a tune and with his children running beside him.

I didn't take much notice of Pocky's warning. We all knew crime went on, and it was pretty obvious that powerful men whose faces we never saw were involved in it. Quennell was always kind and patient as I struggled to remember the sounds of the letters and the awkward way they would change what they said according to which

55

other letters they were with. I was fine with *cat* and *cart*, *mat* and *market*, but I couldn't see why *enough* sounded like *stuff* while *cough* rhymed with *toff*, and I often felt baffled and stupid.

'Don't try to rush it, James,' Quennell would say. 'It takes time, and you're doing well.'

I went for my lessons in the late afternoon, when I'd finished my day's selling and before Quennell went out to do his stint at the lodging-house. He was always alone— but one afternoon as I climbed the narrow stairs beside the baker's shop, I could hear his voice and another one talking quietly in the attic room. I tapped at the door and waited, and when Quennell opened it, I saw a woman rise from the chair I usually sat in. She was dark-haired, wearing a black coat and bonnet that weren't new, but the thing that struck me about her was her eyes. One of them was a deep brown, but the other was almost colourless—a pale, chalky blue like a wall-eyed dog.

'James, this is Mrs Hailstone,' Quennell said. 'An old friend of mine.' He turned to the woman. 'This is James Rivers.' And the pair of them exchanged a glance.

I was instantly uneasy. I wished now that I'd told him straight away that James was only a nickname. Trying to make up for it, I said, 'Mostly, I'm called Joey.'

Both of them were staring at me. 'Fair hair,' the woman murmured.

I flushed under the gaze of Quennell's black eyes and Mrs Hailstone's odd-coloured ones, and said, 'What do you mean? What's going on?'

'Nothing at all,' Quennell said quickly. 'You remind us of someone we used to know years ago, that's all. Just a chance resemblance.'

'Who was he?' I demanded. It had flashed into my head at once that they might be talking about my father. 'You know something, don't you?'

Quennell glanced at the woman with a trace of reproof, and she frowned and said, 'I'm sorry. I shouldn't have mentioned it.'

'No matter,' said Quennell. 'Only a passing acquaintance, anyway. Is it time you were getting back, my dear?'

'Yes.' She was pulling on her grey woollen gloves, smoothing the fingers down as if they were made of kid leather. A lady's gesture, I thought. I'd been in enough big houses to know how servants picked up these manners. 'It's Roper's evening off,' Mrs Hailstone said to Quennell, 'and I don't like to leave the house to Jenkins and Jane—she's such a flighty girl.'

A housekeeper, I thought, as Quennell opened the door to see the woman out. Those gloved hands hadn't had the puffy pinkness of a cook who worked over a hot range. She was a folder of linens and supervisor of maids.

'Back in a moment, James,' Quennell said. His thin little whippet got up as if to follow him, but he told her, 'Stay there, Sadie,' and she lay down obediently.

It was a little time before Quennell came back, and when he did, his pale face looked strained. He sat down at the desk and opened the book we worked from, but his fingers were trembling, and after a few moments he got up and went to the small cupboard. I watched him covertly as he took out the decanter with his back turned to me and poured a little into the small glass. He drank it in two or three slow sips, then put the bottle and glass back. When he sat down again, his dark eyes met mine, and they were glittering with something that looked like tears. He put his forehead in his hand and I tried not to stare at him, but I couldn't help it.

After a few moments, he lifted his head and said unsteadily, 'James. My dear boy. Please forgive me.'

'Nothing to forgive,' I muttered. If he meant the laudanum, that was his business, not mine.

Quennell sighed and sat back in his chair, letting his hands lie in his lap, calmer now. 'The magic potion,' he murmured as if to himself. 'The easer of pain, the bringer of beautiful dreams.' He gave me a sad smile. 'May you never need it, James.' And I did not answer.

9

In the days that followed Mrs Hailstone's visit, I could see something had gone wrong with Quennell. He seemed nervous and uneasy, jumping if a door banged and sometimes getting up to stare through the little window into what he could see of the street below. He was absent-minded about the lessons, and I found it hard to concentrate, and for a few days I didn't go.

Rose pointed out that Quennell might simply be suffering from toothache, but whatever it was, I ought to keep going to my lessons, otherwise I'd forget all I'd learned. 'Go and see him now,' she urged as we sat by the fire one night. 'I know it's late, but it's probably making him feel worse that you've given up coming. Just look in and tell him you'll want a lesson tomorrow as usual.'

'You're nagging,' I said, and she nodded cheerfully. 'That's right,' she said. 'Go on—it won't take long.'

I supposed she was right. I hadn't thought that Quennell might simply be in pain—I'd been too busy imagining that he was up to something that scared him. Something to do with Meachum, perhaps. Or something to do with Mrs Hailstone and that odd visit. I went off through the dark streets, feeling more generous towards him.

Quennell opened the door quickly when I knocked, but his face fell when he saw who I was. 'Ah, James. Do come in. I thought it might be someone about Sadie.'

The whippet wasn't in her usual place on the bed. She wasn't anywhere in the room. I mentally cursed Lucky

Luke, certain that he'd taken her. 'When did she go?' I asked.

'Yesterday.' Quennell sounded wretched. 'She was with me in the market—not when I was working, I'd just gone out for some candles. When I turned round from the stall, she'd gone.'

I nodded. Lucky had told me how it was done. *Smear your hand with liver paste, they'll always come sniffing for that. Then quick into a sack and off.* 'We'll get her back,' I said, 'don't worry.' I'd go and find Lucky Luke right now, I thought. But where? Maybe he'd shifted from the old boat-shed now he was moving up in the world.

'They'll want money,' Quennell said bleakly. 'And I haven't got any, James. If they bring her back and I can't pay, they'll probably kill her.' A small rush of anger overcame him, and he added, 'It's illegal now, you know. Anyone stealing a dog to demand a ransom can get eighteen months' hard labour.'

I whistled. So the gentry had indeed cut up rough. Lucky would know that, so he'd be sticking to poorer people like Quennell. They might not have as much money, but at least they wouldn't go to the police.

'I hoped that something would happen,' Quennell said. 'A plan . . . but I've heard nothing. I'm glad you're coming back, James—you are coming back, aren't you?'

'Yes,' I said. 'That's what I came to tell you. Tomorrow, usual time.'

He nodded. 'I feel I have failed you of late. Tell you what—' He took the book we used from its place on the shelf and handed it to me. 'Take this and do a little revision tonight—it will refresh your mind. Bring it with you tomorrow.'

'*Take* it?' I was staggered. What would the other coster boys say if they saw me walking through the market with a book under my arm?

Quennell seemed to understand. 'Never be ashamed of your intelligence, James,' he said. 'Shame is the worst enemy. I didn't understand that for a long time, and now I have no pride left. But we won't give up hope.' With his usual courtesy, he opened the door for me. 'Tomorrow I may have some money. God forgive me, but I may have.'

Somehow, I did not want to wonder what he meant.

Outside, the market stalls stood in Wentworth Street like empty skeletons, stripped of their daytime awnings and their piles of goods. Holding the book carefully, I set off towards the river. This was the best time to find Lucky, wherever he might be. During daylight hours, I was too busy, and heaven only knew what he might be up to.

The walls of warehouses were high on either side of me as I went down Dark House Lane to Nicholson's Wharf, and the smell of the river was strong. A single lamp burned by the steps that led down to the jetty where the boathouse used to stand—but even in the half-dark, I could see that it had gone. A few jagged stumps stuck up from the wooden decking, but nothing that could be carried away remained. Splintered timber, no matter how rotten, could always be used as firewood.

Drawn a blank, then. No luck, no Lucky. And nobody to ask. I retraced my way up the lane. As I turned into Lower Thames Street, a dazzling burst of light shone in my face, and my way was blocked by a policeman, his bull's-eye lantern held high.

'And where may you be going?' he demanded.

'Home,' I said. *Shame is the worst enemy*. I had nothing to be ashamed of.

'Oh, yes? And where is that?'

'Sugarloaf Court.'

'Long way off your patch, aren't you?'

'It's only about a mile,' I said.

It was a mistake. 'Oh, a clever boy, are we?' His voice was heavy with sarcasm, and his lamp shifted to pick out the book I held under my arm. 'And what have you got there?'

'A book.' I showed it to him, but kept a firm hold on it.

'Very nice, I'm sure,' the peeler said. 'Cost a bit, too. Where did you get it?'

'Someone lent it to me.'

'That's what they all say.' He unbuttoned his tunic pocket and flipped a notebook open. 'Name?'

'James Rivers.' I shouldn't have told him I lived in Sugarloaf Court. What a fool.

'And who do you reckon *lent* you this book?'

'Mr Quennell.' There could be no harm in saying this—Quill Quennell would vouch for me if they asked. 'He lives above Jarrett's the baker's, in Middlesex Street.'

The policeman wrote it down, then frowned at the words. 'If you've just come from Middlesex Street,' he said, 'you're not on your way home. You've been up to something else.' He was buttoning the notebook back into his pocket. 'It's my belief you pinched that book, and I'm taking you in for—'

I ducked under his outstretched hand and ran. He was after me surprisingly fast for a big man, but he was weighed down by his heavy cape, and I gained on him, sprinting across the road and making for the maze of alleys and courtyards on the far side. I heard the shrill blast of his whistle, and kept going, knowing that every peeler within earshot would be after me. I was heading away from home, but I couldn't help that. I ran on and came to the road that led to London Bridge, crossed it and belted past the Fishmongers' Hall—and then, like a rabbit in sight of a burrow, I knew where I could hide. I ran down Wheatsheaf Alley to the river wall, turned right and dived into Black Raven Alley. I paused there for a moment and listened. There were shouts in the distance, and running footsteps, but they didn't sound close.

I went in through the door with the bell that clanged above my head and groped my way up the dark stairs. Then I hammered on Red Jack's door.

'Who is it?' The voice sounded as if it was close on the other side.

'Joey. Oh, please—'

The door opened, and I tumbled into a room that was dark now, and heavy with the thickness of sleeping people. Red Jack was in his nightshirt, holding a candle that made him look like a giant version of Wee Willie Winkie, the nursery rhyme that Poll used to tell us. 'Come in the back,' he said quietly, and I followed his slippered shuffle to the room at the rear.

A lamp still burned here, glittering in reflected points of light from the glass and porcelain that lined countless shelves on the walls, and I blinked as if I was dreaming. There were little figures as well as plates and glasses— ladies with fans, and shepherdesses, and small gentlemen in white wigs and powder-blue coats.

'My little collection,' Red Jack said as I gazed round. 'What you been up to, boy?'

I told him about the policeman, and about Quennell and Lucky Luke, and I put the book down on the handsome table that had a lace cover over its dark green cloth.

'You don't want to mix with dog-finders and that sort,' said Red Jack. 'You're a coster, Joey. A cut above all that.'

'It's just I'd like to get Quennell's dog back for him,' I said. 'He's been good to me.' I was pretty sure my lessons should have cost a lot more than a penny.

Red Jack sighed. 'Proper little knight in shining armour, aren't you,' he said. 'I don't know where your pal is, I don't have any truck with people like that. But I hear he goes around with the dog-meat man that lives in Half Moon Passage. You'd best ask there. But for Pete's sake don't try it tonight,' he added. 'Just get yourself home and stay there. And leave that book where it is. The peelers won't be looking for a boy who's empty-handed.'

I glanced at the book with regret. I'd been looking forward to showing it to Rose and reading the words I knew.

'If you get stopped, tell 'em you're called William Green and you've been here all evening with me,' Red Jack said. 'I'll back you up if they come here, but most likely they won't. There's more criminals out there than you, boy.'

He put the book into a top drawer of the massive sideboard, then went to the window and listened. 'Sounds quiet out there,' he said. 'Off you go, boy. And be careful.'

10

I made an early start the next morning, planning to sell a couple of loads as soon as I could, then hunt down George Bolsover, the dog-meat man. He'd know where I could find Lucky. It would be great to go for my lesson with Quennell and have the dog with me—and I'd pick up his book from Red Jack, too. Pity I didn't get to do any work from it, but that could wait. There was plenty of time.

Rose had been cross with me when I got back last night. She'd been worried because I was out so much longer than she'd expected, and she thought I was stupid to get involved with looking for Quennell's dog. 'It's not your business,' she said. 'You can't stop people getting in a mess—they made it, and it's up to them to get out of it. And now look what you've done—got yourself in trouble with the peelers, and all for nothing.' We'd argued a bit, and I was sorry about that. Tonight, I'd take her out somewhere, just to make up for it.

Coming down Middlesex Street with the load of new season's oranges I'd bought from Sammy, I saw a crowd outside the baker's shop. I joined them and craned my neck to see what they were looking at—and saw Mrs Jarrett pouring out a hysterical story.

'I heard the dog whining, see—Sadie, he calls her—so I thought, oh, she's back, then. She'd been pinched and he was that worried about her, but I thought his door might be shut and the dog couldn't get in—he always sleeps heavy in the mornings. So I went up.' She gave a

65

shuddering sob, and the tutting women who stood round her drew closer. 'The door wasn't shut, it was standing open, and he was at his desk, with his head down on it like he'd gone to sleep there, and the little dog was beside him, whining. Shaking like a leaf, she was. It was still half dark, so I didn't see it for a moment.' She put her hands to her face, and the women clucked and patted her. 'A blooming great knife sticking out of his back. Blood everywhere.' She burst into tears.

I felt cold and sick. My carefree plan for the day fell into ruins, mocking me for having made it. Quennell was dead. I was too late, Lucky had been back—but Lucky wouldn't kill anyone. He was a rogue, but not that sort of rogue. Not a murderer. My legs felt as if they had turned to water.

Two men came down the stairs with Mr Jarrett, all of them looking serious and important. 'He's a goner, all right,' one said. 'Stiff as a board. He's been dead a good few hours.'

Mrs Jarrett was still talking through her tears. 'Who'd do a thing like that? It gave me a fair turn, finding him—' Then she saw me, and her face changed. 'He was there last night,' she said. 'That boy with the oranges. I went to close the shutters, last thing, and there he was, crossing the street. He was often up at Mr Quennell's.'

The crowd turned all its faces towards me, and I backed away. A drizzle of rain was falling, and confusion raged in my mind. The police were looking for me already. I'd even told them I'd been to see Quennell. I took another step back, and hands grabbed at me. 'Just you wait a minute,' a man said. A fine drizzle was falling, and my foot slipped on the wet cobbles as I tried to duck away. My heavy load of fruit tilted and began to spill, and in desperation I pushed the whole shallow away from me, heaving the strap from round my neck, letting it go. The good oranges were rolling on the ground, and I was running again, as I had done last night.

A few men set out after me, but they didn't come far, and even in my panic, I knew why. Any minute now, the police would turn up, and no coster would want to get dragged into their investigations. Better to say you'd seen nothing and knew nothing—but that wasn't to say they weren't interested. They'd be looking for me, all right. Costers had their own justice. I'd seen a man who thieved someone else's stock fined ten bob, and no argument. 'Borrow it if you haven't got it,' said the men Red Jack had sent, 'or you'll take a beating.'

I made myself slow to a walk, although my legs were shaking with the urge to run and hide. People noticed someone running—specially the police. But where could I go? Not home to Sugarloaf Court, that was for sure. When they heard Mrs Jarrett's story, they'd be round there. Poor Rose—she'd be frantic. My looks were against me, too— there weren't many coster boys with sandy-fair hair like mine, we were a darkish lot on the whole. I couldn't go back to Poll and Curly, and I daren't show my face in the market. My shallow was gone, and so was all my stock. I was on my own. I walked on through the drizzle, heading away from Middlesex Street, with no plan.

Two policemen came towards me, their dark capes shiny with rain, and my heart thudded with fear, but they were chatting to each other and went on without looking at me. They hadn't heard yet what had happened. I crossed the road and skirted round the high walls of the Tower, which didn't make me feel any better. They used to cut people's heads off in there, and stick them on spikes for everyone to see. Nowadays they just hanged you in some common prison.

I came to the river and turned left, walking downstream towards St Katharine's Docks where the big ships lay at their wharves. The slow, grey Thames comforted me a little with its indifference. It did not care what some boy called James or Joey had done or not done. It would not drag me to jail and to the long words of lawyers in some courtroom and to a noose about my neck. It would not kill me.

It killed some people, though, I thought. Whether they fell into its murky water by accident or through someone else's purpose, people drowned. Just ahead of me was the slipway where the floating bodies were brought in. It was a good trade, Lucky Luke had told me once—the men who went out with their nets and gaffs often found money in a sodden pocket, or a ring on a finger. A rain-washed notice board stood by the slipway with a couple of bits of paper pinned to it, and I stopped to stare at the letters painted along the top. PERSONS—that was plain enough, but I guessed at the other two words and knew they were probably right. FOUND DROWNED. *Well done, James,* Quennell would have said. A sob gathered in my chest as I thought of his gentle smile, and for a few minutes I leaned against the notice board and wept. Then I rubbed my eyes with my rain-wet sleeve and turned away. There was no helping the dead—it was myself I must look after now.

I walked on, looking over the wall at the river and its muddy foreshore and occasionally glancing round to make sure I wasn't being followed. After a while I saw a group of men below me, making their way through the mud. They wore heavy clothes that were plastered with muck, and each one carried a sack and a long pole with an angled blade at the end. Toshers, I thought. Sewer-hunters, hoping to find coins and valuables that had dropped through city gratings and been washed down here in the flow of rainwater and sewage.

An idea came to me. Nobody would look for me in a sewer-mouth. When these men went in to start their hunting, I would follow them, just far enough to be safely hidden until the evening with its sheltering darkness—though I wasn't sure what I would do then. I found a flight of weedy steps that led from a gap in the wall to the foreshore, and went carefully down, my feet slipping a bit. The men were ahead of me, but they had stopped where a stream of grey water ran across the beach, and there was a flicker of light among them as they lit candles, helping each other to fix them into lanterns that were strapped to their chests. That way, they'd see where they were going and have their hands free. I went up to them, and they turned and stared at me.

'I was wanting to shelter for a bit,' I said. 'Can I come in with you?'

'Don't be stupid,' said one of the men. 'Our job ain't for kids.'

I looked past him at the tunnel entrance and saw that it was blocked by a brick wall a little way inside the entrance, with a heavy iron door hanging in the centre of it. 'How do you get in, anyway?' I asked.

'You don't,' the man said flatly. 'Just go back where you came from, sunshine, and don't say you saw us. There's a five-pound fine if we get caught.'

'I won't tell anyone.' I stood there in the rain, hands shoved in my pockets. 'It's just—I've nowhere to go.'

Another man said more kindly, 'Look, son, it's not safe in there. All right for us, we know what we're doing—but there's places where the bricks are that rotten, you put your hand on one to steady yourself and you could bring the whole roof down.'

'And you got to watch for the flush,' a third added. 'That's when they open the sluice-gates up in the city and the water comes roaring down, fills the tunnels. If you don't know the escape-ledges you're a goner. And there's the rats. Big as tom-cats, some of 'em.'

I gave up. I watched while the men made their way to the tunnel entrance, and saw the first one bend down to grasp the bottom edge of the hanging door. He heaved it up and held it while the others ducked under, then went in himself, and the heavy iron flap fell back into place with a clang that reverberated through the hidden passages inside.

I walked across the slimy stones to the tunnel mouth and crouched down under the brick arch in the small space by the wall where the stream of stinking water ran out from under the iron door. At least I was sheltered from the worst of the rain, and nobody could see me from the road above. I rested my back against the rough bricks and hugged my knees, staring across the river and waiting for the time to pass.

11

T he chill of my wet clothes seemed to spread to my brain, and I lost all sense of passing time—there was only the damp, cold air and the stink of sewage and the cramped ache of my limbs. The tide turned and the river's water began to creep across the foreshore towards me as the sky darkened, and I knew I must move soon. The men would come out before the rising water flooded into the sewer, and I didn't want them to find me still here. I got up, shivering, and walked back to the steps.

I still dared not go back to the city, so I turned right and walked on. After a while, the wall gave way to rough grass and reeds, and the road curved away inland, leaving a sandy path by the river. I followed this, a bit unnerved by the emptiness of it all. With no buildings round me, the sky seemed vast, reaching right down to the water and its low banks, and I wondered how people lived here.

I walked for a long way, and the light ebbed from the sky—then I came to a boatyard. I could smell the fragrant sharpness of sawn wood in the half-dark, and I made my way towards the shapes of the boats. The nearest one was chocked up on baulks of timber, the planking of its sides incomplete, but underneath it was a soft litter of wood-shavings. After the hard, stinking shelter of the sewer-mouth, it was as welcome as a feather bed, and I crept in and curled up like a dog. My limbs began to warm, and I slept.

71

When I woke, it was pitch dark, and very quiet. My stomach was aching with hunger, and I realized almost with surprise that the last thing I'd eaten was a slice of bread and jam with Rose in the dark of the early morning. It seemed impossible that it was the same day—it belonged to a vanished past.

I sat up, almost cracking my head on the underside of the boat above me, and tried to think what to do. One possibility, of course, was to go to the police and tell them the whole story, hoping they'd believe me. But why should they? According to Mrs Jarrett, I was the last person to see Quennell alive. A small voice of common sense argued that no murderer would have admitted to the police on that very night that he'd borrowed a book from the man he was supposed to have killed, but I couldn't trust the police to follow this line of reasoning. Their job was to find a culprit and a case that would stand up in court. One coster boy was much like another as far as they were concerned, and they thought we were all rogues and robbers because we gave short weight sometimes and our half pints of prawns didn't always hold half a pint. No, I daren't go to the peelers.

Somewhere near me, a couple of cats yowled and spat, making me jump. I desperately wished I wasn't alone. Even the doss-house would be better than this awful emptiness. I'd never been alone in my life, and it scared me stiff.

I crept out from under the boat and stood up. Then, without consciously deciding what I was going to do, I picked my way between trestles and timber and half-built boats, making for the road. And there, after a second's hesitation, I turned left and began to walk back to the city.

It was mad, of course. The nearer I got to home, the more risk there was of being spotted and arrested. My hands were pushed deep into my jacket pockets and I crossed my fingers, praying for luck. I was the only person on the empty road, and I was glad to come to buildings, though there was no comforting maze of alleyways yet. My best hope of refuge was Red Jack, though I couldn't have gone running there in broad daylight this morning; it was the wrong way, through the busy centre where the police were always thick on the ground. But I might try for it now, if I couldn't get home.

I came to familiar territory again, passing the Mint, where they made the money that we had to work so hard to earn—I never understood that—and skirted round the Tower, then lost courage. The road was dauntingly wide here, and I could see a couple of policemen on the far side. I ducked across the street and dived into the alley beside the goods yard then went through the arch under the railway. I was dangerously near Sugarloaf Court—but there was just a chance that nobody was watching. I wanted more than anything in the world to be back with Rose, no matter what the risk.

Someone was coming towards me—a dark shape in the shadowed alley, a rattle of wheels over cobbles. And a dog. I tried to duck into a doorway, but I'd been seen. My arm was grabbed, a face was close to mine.

'Pete's sake, Joe, where've you been?'

It was Pocky Dan.

'Hiding,' I said. The relief of seeing him made me feel weak all over.

'You can't go home, the place is stiff with peelers. Get in the barrow.'

'What?'

'Hurry up.' He was heaving up the canvas that covered the folded booth of the Punch and Judy show. 'Climb under here. Pull your feet up.'

I did as I was told, lying flat in the narrow space.

Wooden props cut into my chest and legs, and the heavy canvas pressed down on me so closely that I thought I'd suffocate. Pocky picked up the barrow's shafts, tilting me head-downward so my face was jammed into the tailboard of the barrow, and started off. The jolting of the wooden wheels over the cobbles was hideously uncomfortable, but I was in no state to complain.

After a few minutes the jolting stopped, and I heard a loud voice ask, 'What have you got there?' I held my breath, knowing it was a policeman.

'Punch and Judy show,' Pocky said cheerfully, and added in the squawky voice of Punch, 'Good evening, Mr Policeman! It's very nice to meet you!'

'No need to be cheeky,' said the policeman. 'Where do you live?'

'Goulston Court.'

'And what's your name?'

'Daniel Benson.'

I'd never known Pocky's other name before. I wondered if he'd made it up. There was a pause, and I could imagine the policeman writing it down. Then he said, 'All right. On your way.'

The barrow began to move again, and this time it didn't stop until Pocky put the shafts down and said, quietly and close to my ear, 'You can come out now.'

I wriggled backwards and felt for the ground with one foot, then the other, and stood up. It was good to breathe the cold night air after the hot, stuffy ride.

Pocky led the way into a candle-lit room where children lay sleeping, close-packed in a couple of beds. Kate looked up from where she sat by the fire—and so, to my astonishment, did Poll.

'Joey!' She jumped to her feet and hugged me as she hadn't done since I was a little kid. 'Oh, Joey, I've been that worried. I knew the peelers hadn't got you, or they wouldn't still be hanging round the place, but I couldn't think where you were.'

I started to tell her, but I saw Kate getting a half-loaf out of the cupboard, and my mouth watered so much with hunger that I couldn't say any more. Kate handed me a thick slice with some cheese, and I thought I'd never tasted anything so delicious.

'You're not the only one in trouble,' Poll said as I ate. 'Curly's been arrested.'

'What for?'

'A man in the pub was going on about how you were supposed to have killed poor old Quennell,' Poll said. 'And Curly flared up, told him to shut his trap. And the bloke didn't, so Curly took a swing at him. Well, that started a fight—you know the way he is. The peelers came, and he turned round and socked one of them as well. It took four of them to get the handcuffs on him, so people said.' She was frowning, and I could see she was more upset than she'd let on. 'They reckon he'll get eighteen months. Two years, maybe, with his record.'

I put my hand over hers. She'd had a tough time with Curly, but she'd have a tougher one without him.

Poll gave a little sigh. 'Stupid, isn't it, sticking to a man who's no good to you. I don't know why I stayed so long. But you do somehow, don't you? The father of your kids . . . ' Her eyes met mine and she looked away quickly, and I thought, *she still won't tell me.*

'We'd been up at a birthday party,' Kate put in. 'Big house in Clerkenwell. And coming back, we met Rose, and Poll was with her. They came in for a cup of tea, then Rose said she'd get back to be with the little ones. And your ma's still here.' She smiled at Poll. 'It's nice to get acquainted.' She was cutting me another thick slice of bread as she spoke. 'And Pocky went out to see if he could spot you.'

'I've never been more glad to see anyone,' I said. What good friends they were, these two.

Poll stood up and pulled her shawl about her. 'I must go.'

'Wait till I make sure there's nobody about,' said Pocky. He went out of the door with the brown-patched terrier at his heels, and Kate said, 'You stay here, Joe. You're safe with us.'

I thanked her, knowing that my words weren't enough, then looked at Poll. 'There's things I want to ask you.'

She gave me an awkward smile and said, 'There'll be lots to talk about once all this is over.'

Pocky came back and reported that it was all clear outside, and Poll went out. The dog curled up on the rug and I said to it, 'Shift over a bit—make some space for me.'

But Kate said, 'You'll freeze, Joe. Come in with Dan and me, there's enough room.'

I crept in at Pocky's side, gratefully. After this nightmare day of running and hiding, it was wonderful to be part of a warm family. Even if it wasn't mine.

12

Pocky's family—maybe I should start calling him Dan, I thought—got up late by coster standards. They didn't have to make a trip to a wholesale market before dawn, so they could take their time over putting on their clothes and getting some breakfast organized. Sarah took a couple of the younger children with her to buy loaves, and took the dog as well, while Kate was helping the smallest ones get dressed. All the children wore tawdry bits of stage costume, striped and bright-coloured, with an old jacket or shawl for warmth.

I was a stranger to their world, and I watched as if they were chattering birds with bright, rather tatty feathers. Their work wasn't like mine, but I could see that it was work all the same, bringing Punch and his friends and enemies alive again and again for the people who watched. They had brought it alive for me, many times, and ever since I was small, Punch had seemed a bit like Curly, exploding with temper and yet never seeing that people thought he was dreadful. To both of them, life was a rough old business and you battered your way through it as best you could, and never said you were sorry.

Munching bread and jam and sipping hot coffee, I went on thinking about it. The sausages, the constable, the hangman—my mind flinched away from that. The baby, hurled to the ground in its long clothes, poor Judy whose ghost wandered and wept. All of them came true because these cheerful people took their puppets and their folded stall into the markets or the great houses and showed the watching audience a different world.

'Better get started,' Dan said when the loaves had been eaten and the coffee cups rinsed in a bucket of water. 'Don't go out, Joe. I'm sorry you'll be on your own all day, but at least it's safe.'

'Lock the door when we've gone,' Kate said. 'And if anyone knocks, don't answer.'

I promised I wouldn't.

When they'd all gone out, I sat down at the table with my head in my hands. Hours of empty time lay ahead, and I had nothing to do but think. Again and again I went through all that had happened to me, trying to find some scrap of fresh insight that might make sense of it. I wondered what had happened to Quennell's dog now that her master was dead, and mentally stood again in that attic room with its shelves of books and the little cupboard that contained the decanter of red liquid. I thought of Mrs Hailstone, too, and the way her odd-coloured eyes had surveyed me. She and Quennell had known something about me, that was obvious. And they had denied it. Why?

I couldn't ask Quennell now, and Mrs Hailstone had vanished into whatever mystery she came from. I was stuck here with my questions, and there was nothing to do but follow them round and round like a rat in a cage. If I'd been free to leave this room, I'd have gone to see Poll, and not left until I made her tell me who my father was and why she'd kept it secret all this time. But I wasn't free.

Time dragged agonizingly slowly. By midday, the sun had moved behind the brewery chimney that gave out its rich, malty smell, and there were hours still left to go. I was hungry, but there was nothing to eat. Kate had said she'd come back at dinner time if she could, but I knew it wasn't a promise. I put my head down on my arms.

78

I must have slept, because the sound of footsteps outside jolted me from a broken dream. My heart thumped in alarm—but in the next moment I knew who it was, and smiled. I'd have known those whispering, half-giggling childish voices anywhere. I opened the door before Meg and Stevie had even tapped on it, and they stared up at me, important and excited.

'We brought you these,' Meg said, pushing a big bundle at me.

'Come in, quickly.' They came tumbling into the room, and Stevie tugged an apple from his pocket, and a rather battered ham sandwich wrapped in newspaper. 'They're from Rose,' he said, then looked round the room. 'Why are you here?'

'It's a bit difficult to explain,' I said. 'Did anyone see you come in?'

'No.' Meg shook her head firmly. 'We came out the back and over the wall. And I looked before I came in here, but no one was watching.' She understood more of what was going on than Stevie did. I was clutching the bundle she'd given me, and she explained. 'It's so you can go out, Rose said. Dressed up.' She pressed her hands against her mouth, suppressing another giggle, as I untied the clothes and shook them out.

There was a dark blue wool dress, fairly grubby, a petticoat and a dilapidated bonnet, all wrapped in a knitted grey shawl that had a good few holes in it. I saw at once what Rose meant, and grinned at the children as I held the dress up against me. 'Nobody will know me in this, will they!' I said.

Meg's giggles broke through, but Stevie was serious as usual. 'You look funny,' he said.

'Yes.' I ruffled his hair. 'We're having a funny time just now.'

'A man brought your shallow back,' said Meg.

'Marvellous! Who was he, do you know?'

She shook her head. 'When are you coming home?'

'Soon,' I promised. And hoped it was true.

When the children had gone, I locked the door again, then ate the ham sandwich and the apple. After that, I looked more carefully at the blue dress. It was grease-stained and old, but it was a good size, big enough to cover all of me but the toes of my boots. I didn't like the thought of pulling it over my head and shoving my arms into the sweat-stiffened sleeves, but I had no choice. This was my only way of escape.

The sun was well past the brewery chimney now, dipping behind the roofs in the cold sky. It would be frosty tonight. I took off my jacket and trousers, untied my neck-scarf and stripped off my waistcoat and shirt, then put on the petticoat and tied its waist-string, and hauled the dress over my head. It felt tight round the shoulders but it hung loose everywhere else, and my bare legs felt strange without the warm corduroy that always encased them. I toyed with the idea of putting my trousers on again under the skirt, but abandoned it. Someone was bound to notice—and anyway, it was already hard enough to walk in the long dress without it clinging to thick trousers as well. I found the folds of material tangling themselves between my knees as I crossed the room and back, and saw for the first time why women lifted their skirts free of their feet if they were in a hurry. Even going slowly, walking was quite a tricky business. I found I had to move with shorter steps, letting the dress swing from my hips. I practised for quite a long time, and the sky began to darken. Soon, I could risk going out.

I draped the shawl round my shoulders and put the bonnet on. It was made of black straw, with a faded cotton violet at one side, and when I tied its ribbons under my chin, it hid my hair completely. I stared into the cracked mirror on the mantelpiece. With my fair skin that hadn't managed to grow a beard yet, I looked amazingly girlish. In the ordinary way, I'd have been quite embarrassed by my feminine appearance, but nothing was ordinary now. I folded my own clothes carefully and left them on a chair where Dan and Kate would see them when they came in. It would be a mystery to them, but they'd probably work it out. I wished again that I could write properly—I knew Kate could read, and it would have been so handy to leave a note. But that, like so much else, was just a dream. I took a deep breath, and went out.

In the street, I was horribly aware of my chilly bare legs under the clinging folds of the petticoat and skirt, and of my boots that were so big and unwomanly. I took short steps, hoping the dress would hide my toecaps, and kept my head down modestly so that the bonnet would hide my face. Although I'd been brought here in the darkness of the Punch and Judy barrow, I knew where I was. The brewery whose chimney I had stared at for so long lay just past the public wash-house in Goulston Street, north of Aldgate High Street. I headed south, for Grigg's Court, determined to speak to Poll.

I might have been invisible, a shabby girl slipping through the crowd, of no interest to anyone. Even a couple of passing policemen gave me no more than a casual glance, and I began to feel more confident. As I turned into Goodman's Yard and started to walk across it to the next block, a bull's-eye lantern gleamed suddenly from the darkness, lighting me up like a puppet on a stage. I clutched my shawl round me and flung up a hand to shield my face—and the beam was cut off as the policeman closed the glass in front of it. He was standing at the far side, where anyone would go through to Sugarloaf Court, and I was glad I hadn't taken the risk of going to see Rose. Girlish though I looked, I might not stand up to close inspection. Treading as lightly as I could in my solid boots, I crossed the yard and started up the stairs to my old home.

How do women climb stairs? My long dress kept getting under my feet and I trod on it once or twice, and felt the fabric tug at the waist as if it was going to tear. In desperation, I picked up the skirt in both hands and took the rest of the steps two at a time.

The door was locked. I couldn't believe it. Our door had never been locked. We were nearly all costers in this block, and costers didn't steal from each other—not that we had much to steal, anyway. I rattled at the handle, and heard Poll say from inside, 'Who is it?'

'Me. Joey. For Pete's sake—'

The door was opened and I was inside, bathed in candlelight and the good smell of turnip soup.

Poll stared at me, then began to laugh. 'Where did you get those togs?'

'Rose,' I said. 'She sent Meg and Stevie round.'

'What a girl. You struck lucky there. Are you hungry?' Poll was always practical.

'Not half,' I said. 'Where are the kids?'

'Bobby's out at the pub with his friends and the little ones are selling walnuts. I let them keep the money they make.' She ladled out a bowl of soup and cut a slice of bread while I took my bonnet off and pushed my fingers through my hair. 'Curly got two years,' she said. 'He was up in court today.'

I blew on my first spoonful and looked at her. If she was upset, she hid it well.

'I'll sell Captain,' she went on. 'He's too much for the kids to manage on their own, though Bobby thinks he can. Cart as well. Go back to something smaller.'

'Once I'm clear of all this business, I could help you,' I said. 'Run the big cart while Bobby does a smaller one, split the profit.'

Poll shook her head. 'You've got your own life to lead,' she said. 'And you're not going to get out of this in a hurry, not unless the peelers find the bloke who really killed Quennell. And how's that going to happen?'

'I don't know.' But the hot, peppery soup was comforting, and in the familiar room I felt almost safe.

'Anyway, I need the money,' Poll said. 'Curly was behind with the rent. He owed nearly two months. Meachum sent his men round this morning, said now Curly was inside, how was I going to pay it. If I didn't cough up, me and the kids would be out.'

'But that's not fair! It's not your fault.'

Poll shrugged. 'Who ever said life was fair?' It was a question she used to ask when we quarrelled as kids over who had what. 'We'll be all right. Lanky Phil said he'd give me the money for the donkey and cart up front, and he'd sell them on when he could find a buyer. He's a good sort, Phil.' She met my eye squarely, and I suddenly knew that she had liked the tall coster with the easy grin for longer than any of us knew. 'His wife died three years ago when the last kid was born. Remember her? Bessie Peaches, they called her.'

I shook my head. I hadn't come here to talk about Bessie Peaches, though I did remember that curly-haired woman with the pink cheeks. Poll refilled my bowl then sat down again, and there was silence between us while I ate. Then I said, 'You know what I've come for. Tell me, Poll. Please.'

She sighed, tightening her fingers on her folded arms. For a long moment she didn't answer, then she said, 'I reckon you've a right to know. I thought about it all last night. But then, I've thought about it for years. A secret gets to be a hard thing to break when you've kept it a long time.'

I waited.

Poll took a deep breath. 'My first baby died,' she said. 'Charlie, I called him. He lived for three days then he got pneumonia.' She looked at me, knowing what I was thinking. 'Yes, he was Curly's child. We took up together when we were no more than kids, Curly and me. But it's hard, Joey, losing your first one. Nothing to hold in your arms after all those months of feeling it moving inside you, and you're aching with milk. I just cried all the time. But just about a week later, a woman came to the door one night. She was carrying a new-born baby wrapped in a blanket. She asked if I'd take it.'

I didn't say anything, though questions were jumping in my mind.

'I thought it was her child at first, but it wasn't. He'd been born at the big house where she worked—the daughter of the family had got herself into trouble, as they say.' She gave a little shrug. 'I don't see how anyone can think a baby's birth is trouble, but that's the gentry for you. They set a lot of store on being married. It's because they've got money, and they worry about who's going to inherit it. The girl who had this baby wasn't married, and her father was raging mad about it. They kept her shut away until the baby was born, then her father gave orders the child was to be put on the church steps.'

'So it would be taken to the orphanage,' I said. We all knew this happened.

Poll nodded. 'But the woman was soft-hearted. When it came to taking the baby out to leave it on the cold steps, she couldn't do it.'

Things were dropping into place with dizzying speed. 'But how did she know about you?'

'She had relatives lived round here, she said. I asked

who they were, but she wouldn't tell me. Anyway, I took the baby in.'

'And it was me.' I could hardly speak the words.

'Yes.' Poll was determined to finish her story now. 'Curly was dead against it at first. Said he wasn't taking on someone else's kid. But there was money pinned to the shawl you were wrapped in, inside the blanket. A lot of money.'

'How much?'

'Forty pounds.'

I whistled. Forty pounds was enough to feed a family for a year or more. But none of that mattered. I looked at Poll, and grief welled up inside me. 'So you're not my mother,' I said.

She reached out and put her hand over mine. 'Joey, listen. Some other girl gave birth to you, yes. She was called Miss Judith, the woman said. But you were my baby from that day. I fed you like you were my own, and loved you that way, too. Still do.'

Tears pricked at the back of my eyes, and I couldn't say anything.

'The money did Curly no good,' Poll went on, folding her arms again. 'He spent it on booze, got into a habit he never lost. Treated all his friends, had a high old time.'

'Didn't they want to know where it came from?'

''Course they did. And he told them. But you know what Curly's like, always has to be the big man. He made out he'd been chosen to bring up a lord's son. They laughed. It was only my close friends knew about my baby dying, because I hadn't been out since he was born. So when people saw me around with you, and heard Curly's tales, they reckoned I'd had you by some toff and got a bit of money to shut up about it.'

'But—why didn't you tell me?'

Poll sighed. 'The woman was scared. Said if her master

85

found out what she'd done, she'd lose her job, maybe get put in prison for stealing a baby that was meant to go somewhere else. Same went for me, she said. The money was supposed to go to the orphanage. They could demand it back, and you'd get taken away. So I was always frightened I'd lose you. When you got older and started asking questions, I thought if you knew the truth, you might get some notion of wanting to stir things up—find out where you really came from. And I couldn't tell you that, I still can't, because I don't know, only what I've told you. But you might have got discontented, felt you were a cut above being a coster, and that's no way to be happy, Joey. Fretting for something different, you can't enjoy what's all round you.'

I nodded slowly, in a mixture of pity and rage. These toffs had thrown me out like so much rubbish, and Poll, who had been a mother to me as the girl called Miss Judith never was, had lived all these years in fear.

'The way I saw it,' Poll went on, 'they'd rather have had you tucked away in an orphanage. No name, no connection. No fear that you'd turn up like a bad penny. All their secrecy would be for nothing if that happened.'

'But I will turn up,' I said in my anger. 'I'll find out somehow, just you wait, and remind them what they did fifteen years ago. Why shouldn't I?'

'Don't, Joey,' Poll begged. 'What's the point? You'll never find out anyway, there's nothing to go on. And what would be the use?'

Rose had said the same thing when I'd talked to her about my unknown father. It simply didn't matter, she said. But what about him, anyway? I was still no nearer to knowing who he was.

'So my mother was this Miss Judith,' I said, 'but what about my pa? Who was he?'

'I don't know,' said Poll. 'The woman who brought

86

you didn't know, either. Miss Judith would never say who he was, though her parents did everything they could think of to make her tell.'

For the first time, I felt a trace of respect for my unknown mother. 'She must have been brave,' I said. 'Standing up against them.'

Poll got up from the table and went across to delve under the bed in the wall recess. She hauled out her treasure box and carried it back to where we sat. I'd seen inside it before, when I was a kid, and fingered the few precious things she kept there—a lock of Jenny's hair in tissue paper, a tortoiseshell comb that had been her mother's, a dried flower, a shell. And a bit of paper that none of us could read. It was this bit of paper she took out now.

For a moment, Poll stared at it, then she passed it across the table to me. There was still a small safety-pin in the corner of it, rusted now, and the few lines of graceful writing were faded.

'That was with the money,' Poll said. 'Pinned to your shawl. The woman read it out to me. Something about how your proper name was James but she wanted to call you Joey.'

I scanned the lines again, feverishly. Yes, there were the two words that said my different names, though their sloping shapes were different from the printed ones in Quennell's book. But I couldn't make out the rest of it. 'Can I keep this?' I asked—but I saw a shadow cross Poll's face and knew she couldn't part with this treasure. I handed it back and watched her put it away in the small wooden box and turn the key.

'I can nearly read,' I said. 'Mr Quennell was teaching me.'

Poll put the box back under the bed. What treasures did Miss Judith have? I wondered absently. Things that would make Poll's little collection look shabby and poor. One day, perhaps, she would give me that letter. But it would have to be in her own time.

I could see now why I'd been called Lord James as a kid—and I knew, too, that I had every right to call myself James if I wanted to. Much had fallen into place, but there were still big pieces missing, because of the mystery about my father.

'Isn't there *anything* else you can remember?' I begged. 'What about the woman who brought me here? Did you find out her name?'

Poll shook her head. 'She wouldn't tell me.'

'What did she look like?'

'Ordinary. Keeping up appearances, the way servants do. Worn cuffs on her coat, dark clothes. She had funny eyes, though.'

'Funny?' I was jerked into a breathlessness that almost choked me as a mad suspicion presented itself. 'What kind of funny?'

Poll gazed past me into her memories. 'One was dark, but the other was pale blue. Like a wall-eyed dog.'

13

Crossing Aldgate High Street on my way back to Kate and Dan's, I saw a group of lads come out of the pub on the corner, shouting and singing. And among them was Lucky Luke. I paused, because there was a lot I wanted to say to Lucky—but then I realized I couldn't go up to him in my female clothes. He'd roar with laughter, and all the boys he was with would be told who I was, and that was too dangerous. I went on up the street, thinking hard, then glanced over my shoulder.

Lucky caught the glance. 'Wait for me, darling!' he shouted. 'I'll see you home!'

I hurried on, not wanting him to catch up with me while he was still with the others. I realized that looking back had been a rash thing to do. I'd only meant to see if he was coming up this street, but he thought I was a girl, giving him the come-on. There was a lot about this business of being a girl that I hadn't understood.

Lucky shouted goodbye to his friends then came after me—and I knew now what I was going to do. I ducked into an alley and stood still just inside it, waiting. He came round the corner and didn't see me in the dark, and I put my elbow round his neck and held on tight. He choked and gasped beerily, then buckled at the knees, and I said in his ear, 'It's me—Joey. Shut up, don't say anything.'

I felt him stop struggling and cautiously released him.

'Cor, you gave me a fright,' said Lucky. 'No need to cut up rough.' He rubbed his throat, then sketched a gesture at my dress and bonnet. 'What's all this, then?'

'What d'you think?' I asked. 'Every peeler in London's after me, because of Quennell. And I didn't kill him. You know that, don't you?'

'All I know is, he was dead when I got there,' Lucky said. 'I never had you as the murdering sort, though, no more than I am.'

'But you took his dog, didn't you?' I was angry now that poor Quennell's last days had been spent in such unhappiness and worry.

'Well, yes,' Lucky admitted. 'I knew Quennell wasn't worth much, but George got done when the peelers found two spaniels and a poodle locked up in his shed, and I was on my own. Had to come back to the small stuff.'

'So that night—what happened?'

'I took the whippet back. It was late—church bells had gone ten, nobody about. His door was open. That surprised me, I thought he'd be in bed. It's good if they are, people don't have their wits about them much if they've just woken up. But he was at his desk, with his head down like he'd gone to sleep there. I went to give him a little shake, then I saw the knife sticking out of his back. Blood all over the desk—I got it on my hands and my jacket, didn't know what to do. Then the dog starts growling and snarling—'

He paused. Both of us heard the measured tread of footsteps coming down the street.

'Peeler,' I breathed.

The pool of light from the policeman's lantern was coming closer. 'Courting couple,' Lucky whispered. 'And for Pete's sake don't strangle me.'

My face was hidden against his shoulder as the light paused and played briefly over us then went on again. Lucky released me and said, 'Pity you aren't a girl.'

'Forget it,' I said. 'So the dog was snarling.'

'Right. Hackles all up, nose pointing at something

behind the door. *Someone there*, I thought. It was a nasty moment, I can tell you. Couldn't move. Then the bloke makes a break for it. Out from behind the door, past me, off down the stairs.'

'Did you see him? What was he like?'

'He had his head down, didn't want me to see him, of course. Arm across his face.'

'You don't know who he was?'

Lucky shook his head. 'Wish I did,' he said. 'Let us both off the hook, wouldn't it. As it is, I'm in it as deep as you.'

'No, you're not,' I said. 'The police don't know you were there, and they know all about me.'

'The bloke who killed Quennell knows I was there, though,' Lucky said. 'There was a bit of light coming through the window, from the street lamp. He could have got a good look at me before the dog started carrying on.'

'If he was going to have a go at you, he'd have done it straight away,' I pointed out—but Lucky wasn't convinced.

'He was as scared as I was,' he said. 'He went off down those stairs like all the devils of hell were after him. That's a thing, though,' he added. 'His footsteps were kind of uneven—ker-dump, ker-dump, like he limped a bit.'

'That's not much help,' I said. 'There's plenty of people who limp.'

'I know. But I've been thinking—the night-cart was down in Aldgate High Street, just at the crossroads. It's only a step or two from Jarrett's.'

'What about it?' The night-cart emptied the cesspools in the big houses that had inside privies and sewage tanks in the basement.

'There's a bloke works on the cart that limps. Togger Bill, they call him. Used to be in the second-hand clothes trade.'

'And you think he could have—'

'Dunno. But there was no one else about when I came out of Jarrett's, and the cart had moved off down the road.'

I thought about it. Standing there in the dark alley, Lucky and I were both more scared than we'd let on. Neither of us dared go to the police, but until someone else knew what Lucky had seen in Quennell's room that night, there was no hope of any move towards catching the real killer. 'We need help,' I said. And there was only one man I could think of who might be able to do something about it. 'Red Jack. You know the man I mean? He's—' How could I put it? 'He's like a kind of grandfather to all the costers. He sorts things out. He knows people.' I wasn't sure who Red Jack knew, but I'd heard it said that anyone who crossed him would end up floating in the river with his hands tied together. Then I thought of the delicate porcelain figures that lined Red Jack's walls and doubted whether the stories about him could be true.

'I know the geezer you mean,' Lucky said. 'Big bloke, red hair gone grey.' He frowned. 'What's to stop him going to the police if we tell him?'

'He wouldn't,' I said with certainty. 'He's a coster. He lives in—'

'I know where he lives,' said Lucky. 'I used to be right near there when I was in the boathouse.'

'Where are you now?'

'Smithfield way,' he said vaguely, and I knew he wasn't sure if he could trust me.

'Go and see him,' I urged. 'Go and tell him what you've told me.'

Lucky looked at me. 'And if I don't?'

'If you don't,' I said, 'then I will. And he'll wonder why you didn't come yourself. He'll wonder if you were afraid to face him.'

'You mean he'll wonder if I killed Quennell,' said Lucky.

I said nothing, and he sighed. 'You're a tough nut, you are,' he said. But I wasn't going to let him slide off into the shadows again and leave me as the only one being hunted and blamed.

'Go now,' I said. 'It's not far from Smithfield. If you don't, every coster in London will be looking for you.'

'Oh, all right, all right,' said Lucky. 'No need to twist my arm.' He gave me a friendly thump on the shoulder. 'Watch out for yourself, right?'

'And you,' I said.

'I'll be all right,' said Lucky. 'See you.' And he glanced both ways along the street then set off, heading towards the river.

I pulled my shawl about my shoulders and straightened my bonnet, then walked in the other direction, towards Goulston Court and the safety offered by the Punch and Judy man.

14

There was plenty of time the next day to think about what had happened and what Poll had told me. As the hours dragged on in Kate and Dan's room, I went through my meeting with Lucky again in my mind, and wondered if he really had gone to see Red Jack—and I thought, too, of Poll's story.

So you really are a toff, Rose would say. And she'd laugh. All these years, I'd had it wrong, thinking Poll was my mother, suspecting she'd had a fling with some adventuring member of the gentry. I felt ashamed of that thought now, because going out dressed as a girl had taught me something of how vulnerable women were to an advance they couldn't fend off. What if I'd really been a girl when I met Lucky last night? Things would have been very different.

And how different my life would have been if Miss Judith had been married to my father, whoever he was. For the sake of a ring on the finger and words said in church, I had lost all the privilege of being brought up in a big house with servants, of wearing good clothes and going to school, of knowing important, influential men and moving into business on a scale no coster could imagine, perhaps not even Red Jack. I might have been an owner of great ships and all their cargoes. I would have ridden about on a fine horse, or in a carriage.

Would I really have wanted all that? I wasn't sure. At the moment, all I wanted was to be outside, mixing with people in the streets and the markets, selling my fruit and hearing all the latest news and gossip—and above all, to see Rose. The worst thing about this whole business was being shut away from her. I was tempted to put the blue dress on and go looking for her—but the frosty morning sun was very bright, and if some sharp-eyed policeman spotted my boots or my big, raw-knuckled hands, I was done for.

At dinner time Kate came back, bringing me a meat pie. 'Oh, great!' I said—but she sat down opposite me, and there was something about her face that made me bring my hand back from the pie she had put down on the table.

'Bad news, Joe. The boy you met last night—Lucky Luke. They found him this morning, in a cellar near Smithfield. He'd been strangled.'

I stared at her and felt the blood drain from my face.

'I'm so sorry,' Kate said. 'You liked him, didn't you.'

I nodded dumbly. *Watch out for yourself*, he'd said. And then, *I'll be all right*. But he hadn't been all right. Was it my fault, for insisting that he must go and see Red Jack? I got up from the table and stared out of the window at the pale sky of late November, not wanting Kate to see that I was struggling with tears.

Yes, I'd liked Lucky. He was as shifty as a rat that lives as best it can in the dirt and rubbish that other people leave, and he had done things that caused people distress—but who has not? Are any of us innocent? His scrawny grin was in my mind again, and his irreverent cheerfulness, and my grief was mingled with anger that someone out there, some faceless man who could command his evil servants, had killed him like a fly.

'I'll have to go,' said Kate. 'We're doing a show for a birthday party. But I thought you ought to know. Be careful if you go out later, Joe. You can see what this means, can't you?'

'Yes.' I'd be doubly wanted now. As far as the police were concerned, the killer of Quennell was still at large, and had struck again.

It was a long time before I could eat the pie.

When it began to get dark, I put on the dress and shawl and tied the bonnet ribbons under my chin, and went out. Danger nagged at me like the shivery beginnings of a fever, but I told myself I must surely be safe here in the market, among the sellers of common things—tea, candles, wash-leathers, walking sticks—not to mention the piled stalls of clothes and china, and the costers shouting the last of their wares from half-empty barrows. Nobody could strike me down in the middle of the crowd. But I might be watched. Was anyone who they seemed? I glanced with new suspicion at the old man who sold spectacles from a green baize tray, and even at the boy with his packages of rat-poison, and when a hand was pushed into mine from behind, I jumped half out of my skin.

It was Stevie, with Meg at his side, both of them beaming up at me. I picked the little boy up and whispered in his ear, 'Don't say who I am, Stevie. It's a sort of game. Don't say my name to anyone.'

'I know,' said Stevie. 'Rose told us.' Then he pointed. 'She's over there.'

Rose was coming towards me. She was carrying my shallow, laden with almonds and walnuts. Her face brightened when she saw me, and she reached up to give me a kiss, our bonnets colliding absurdly. I put my arm round her shoulders and said quietly, 'You heard about Lucky?'

Rose nodded. She made her way across to an empty shop doorway where we wouldn't be overheard, then looked up at me. 'What are you going to do?' she asked.

Dear Rose. It was so like her not to waste words on

telling me how worried she'd been. I poured out Poll's story of how I had been brought to her as a baby by the woman with odd eyes, and she listened intently, head a little on one side like a robin waiting for crumbs.

'And you think it's the same woman as the one who came to see Quennell?' she asked.

'I can't be sure,' I said. 'But I've never seen anyone else with eyes like that.'

'Nor have I,' Rose agreed. 'You'll need to try and find her, once all this is over.'

'I need to find her now,' I said. I told her what Lucky had found when he went to Quennell's room, and about the man who had bolted out. 'And Lucky's been killed. It can only be because of what he saw.'

'Got to be,' said Rose, nodding. 'But what I don't understand is why anyone would kill Quennell in the first place. It's not as if he had any money.'

'No. But I think he was up to something. After Mrs Hailstone came, he was all worried and jumpy. And the last time I saw him—that time when you sent me round there—he was fretting about having to pay to get his dog back. And he said he might have some money the next day. "God forgive me," he said, "but I might have." Mrs Hailstone's the only person I can think of who'd know what that meant.'

'Makes sense.'

'And—I know it sounds stupid, but I keep having this feeling it all ties together. The way they looked at each other when he introduced me. "This is James Rivers." She said something about me having fair hair, but they both clammed up when I asked what she meant.'

'Where did you get *Rivers* from?' Rose asked.

'It was Meachum, the time he rode over Stevie. "You think I'll keep Lord Rivers waiting?" he said. And when Quennell asked my name at the doss-house, I felt so bad

97

about being there, I wanted to keep my real name out of it—not that Curly's name is mine, anyway. So I said the first thing that came into my head.'

'Well, that explains it,' said Rose. 'If they both pricked their ears up at the sound of the name, it must be someone they know. Probably the same man Meachum knows. There can't be all that number of Lord Riverses about. It sounds to me as if he's the spider at the middle of this web. So you'd better go and see him.'

'*What?*' The idea terrified me. If Meachum was worried about keeping him waiting, then Lord Rivers was a man of unimaginable power. 'I can't do that.'

'Yes, you can. You don't have to march up and ask if he's a murderer—just say you're looking for a Mrs Hailstone. Even if he sets the dogs on you, you might learn something. What have you got to lose?'

'My life, I suppose,' I said, with a sort of smile that didn't come off very well.

'But you'll never have your life unless we do something,' Rose pointed out. 'And what if they think Lucky told you what he saw? You'll be the next one found dead.' For a moment, her bravery cracked a little and she ducked her head towards my shoulder, hampered by the cumbrous shallow. I took it from her and put it on the ground, then gathered her to me.

'Peeler coming,' reported Meg, who had been keeping a look-out. We adjusted our bonnets and shawls, and I put a hand on my hip, back turned to the street, hoping we looked like two women in conversation.

The policeman walked by.

Rose looked up at me. There were tears in her eyes, and I wiped them away with my finger and kissed her. It was worth any risk if we could be together again, in our own home. 'So how do I find out where Lord Rivers lives?' I asked.

'Ask a cabbie,' said Rose.

I thumped myself on the forehead for not thinking of it, knocking my bonnet sideways. Cabbies spent their time taking the gentry to their houses—of course they'd know.

'Call yourself a toff!' said Rose. She straightened my bonnet and took my hand. 'Come on. There's a coffee stall by the cab-rank—the cabbies all get round there while they're waiting for a fare. I'll do the asking. Your voice doesn't sound like a girl's.'

I put the strap of the shallow round my own neck, and we set off, Stevie holding my hand. A woman stopped and asked for some almonds, and I was so scared of replying that my voice went squeaky. She didn't seem to notice anything, though, and went on her way.

At the coffee stall, I stood back with Meg and Stevie while Rose did the enquiring.

'My sister heard they were wanting a kitchen maid at Lord Rivers's house,' she said. 'Do you know where it is?'

'Rivers? Finsbury Place, isn't it,' one of them said, bulky in his driving coat with the three layers of cape on the shoulders.

'Past the livery stable, third on the left,' another man agreed. He glanced at Rose and added, 'I wouldn't think your sister's got much chance though, dear. They pick and choose, that lot.'

'I told her she'd be lucky,' Rose agreed. 'Still, no harm in trying, is there?'

She came back looking pleased with herself, and I said, 'I never knew you had a sister.'

'I haven't,' said Rose.

We walked on for a bit, then stopped as if by mutual agreement, knowing it was dangerous to go any nearer to Sugarloaf Court. We looked at each other, and Rose said, 'You take care.'

'You, too.' I didn't know where the danger might end. We gripped each other's hands tightly, then I bent to kiss the children. Rose took the shallow from me, and our eyes exchanged a long glance. She turned away, and I watched the three of them until they'd gone round the corner. Then I walked back up the road, heading for Finsbury.

I knew the area well from selling round the big houses, but I'd never looked at the brass plates that had the owners' names on them. Like the servants who polished them, I'd just thought they were part of the house, a decoration like the scrolled tops to the wrought-iron railings. Now, I stopped and stared at each one, working hard to recall the letters and sounds that Quennell had taught me.

Third on the left, the cabbie had said—but I wanted to be sure I wasn't going to blunder into the wrong house. The first plate had a long name that was in two parts joined by a little line—a hyphen, Quennell had called it— so I ignored that. The next one was wrong as well, but I spelt it out all the same. ARCHIBALD. Then I came to the third house, and the six familiar letters that I had written in the attic room jumped out at me.

RIVERS.

I looked over my shoulder. There was nobody about. Spotlessly white steps led to the imposing front door, but I knew I couldn't go up there. Maybe Rose might have done, acting out some fairytale about an imagined sister, but I dared not risk the bright gaslight of the hall and the glare of an officious butler. Safer to go down the area steps to the servants' quarters.

A uniformed maid answered to my knock, opening the door only just wide enough to see who stood there. 'No beggars,' she said, and attempted to shut it again.

I put my hand on it. 'I'm not a beggar. I just want to know something. This is *Lord* Rivers's house, isn't it?' The brass plate had simply said RIVERS, and I needed to be sure I was in the right place.

'Yes.' She was staring at me oddly, and I realized I hadn't thought about my voice. For the last few months it had been difficult, often cracking to a deep bass. 'You'll have to go,' she said. 'I'm not allowed to speak to callers.'

'What is it, Jane?' A woman's voice came from behind the maid, and the glow of a lamp came closer—no gaslight down here.

The maid looked nervously over her shoulder as the thin figure in a black dress approached, white apron and ruffled cap bright in the lamplight. 'All right, Jane, I'll deal with this,' the woman said.

The maid turned away, and the lamp was held high, to illuminate my face—and I found myself staring into the oddly-matched eyes of Mrs Hailstone.

15

I don't know which of us was the most afraid. She knew me at once. Her hand flew to her mouth, and I thought she was going to go screaming back into the house and say there was a murderer at the door.

'Please,' I said, 'I mean you no harm. I need to speak to you. About Mr Quennell.'

Colour had flooded to her pale face, but she rode the shock well. 'Wait for me in the square,' she said quietly. Then she raised her voice, speaking for those in the kitchen behind her to hear. 'Lord Rivers does not allow hawkers, canvassers, or visitors. Kindly leave the premises at once.' And she shut the door so firmly that I could hardly believe it was meant as a pantomime.

I climbed the steps to the pavement and walked back to Finsbury Square at the end of the street. Children came here early in the morning to haggle for watercress from the growers who brought it in. I'd seen them before dawn, washing the bunches of green leaves in the fountain. Nobody here now. I sat down on a bench and wondered if Mrs Hailstone would come. Her promise could have been a ruse to get rid of me while she went to her master to tell him who had been at the door. I was wanted by the police for the murder of Quennell, probably of Lucky as well. I got up from the bench and moved to the shadow of some evergreen shrubs, looking through their branches at the gateway through which she would come. If she wasn't alone, I'd run for it.

But she was alone. She looked very thin, clutching her

shabby black coat at the throat and staring about her. Very thin and very scared. I came out from the bushes and walked towards her.

'James,' she said. Her voice was hardly more than a whisper.

'Yes.'

She swayed a little, and I was suddenly concerned for her. I put my hand under her elbow and said, 'Come and sit down.'

On the bench beside me, she sat with her gloved hands in her lap, tightly clenched.

'It was brave of you to come,' I said. 'The police think—'

'I know what they think. But you didn't kill Eddie.'

'Eddie?'

'Quill Quennell, as you knew him.'

'Who did?'

'I don't know. All I know is why.' She paused, then asked, 'How did you find me?'

It took some time to explain, and at the end of it she gave a little sigh and said, 'You're a clever boy. As I might have expected.'

It was Rose who was clever, I thought. But a big question was burning in my mind. 'Were you working for Lord Rivers when I was born? Did I come from—'

'Yes. I've been twenty years with the family.'

'Then—'

'Miss Judith is Lord Rivers's daughter. He is your grandfather.'

I stared at her, appalled and yet excited, trying to take in what this meant. 'But Mr Quennell—Eddie—'

Mrs Hailstone sighed. 'I blame myself,' she said. 'I knew it wouldn't work, I tried to tell him, but he was so desperate.' Tears came to her eyes and she fumbled for a handkerchief. 'I'm not making sense to you, James,

103

I'm sorry.' She took a deep breath. 'You see, Eddie took opium.'

'I know. He told me.' Pocky Dan had told me, too.

'It's very expensive. Far too dear for him to afford at chemist's prices, in the quantity he used. But somebody supplied it cheaper, on condition he did certain little favours.'

'Like working in the lodging-house.'

She looked at me. 'You know more than I thought. But there were other things, too. People spied on, tales told. He hated it. But he couldn't break the habit. He dreamed of being free, but it was just a dream. Then you came to the lodging-house and gave your name as James Rivers. Eddie knew what I'd done, he'd always known. And he knew your existence was a secret that Lord Rivers wouldn't want known. He thought—poor Eddie—if he wrote a letter to him, saying he knew of your identity, Lord Rivers would pay him to keep quiet.'

'Oh, I *see*!' *I may have some money tomorrow* . . . But then came the piece of understanding that sickened me. 'But instead—' I couldn't say it. Lord Rivers, who was my grandfather, had caused Quennell to be killed. So much more effective than paying. I stared at Mrs Hailstone and was speechless.

'Yes.' She looked down at the handkerchief she clutched in her gloved hands. 'I didn't think Eddie would write the letter. He was a kind man, but not a brave one. He didn't realize, of course, just what danger he'd be in. And neither did I.' Her glance met mine. 'Lord Rivers called me in one morning. The post had come, and he had this letter in his hand. I recognized Eddie's writing. He asked me to recall a certain event that happened nearly fifteen years ago. The child . . . Was I perfectly certain I had carried out my orders? For just one moment, I hesitated. Then I said I had, of course—but I'm not a good liar, James. He stared at me, and I felt that he could see right through me. He said that would be all, and I went out of the room. The next day, he gave me my notice. I'm to leave at the end of the month.'

And Quennell had been brushed away like a troublesome fly. A quiet word with the useful Meachum, and a man had been deployed to tidy up this nuisance. I could see it all now. The man reported that Lucky had seen him and so, after a search that took a couple of days, Lucky was disposed of as well. Did Mrs Hailstone know this? I told her, and she nodded bleakly.

'I heard. Dear God, where will it end?'

I could see only too well where it would end. 'If the police don't get me, my grandfather will,' I said. Poll had been right, and so had Rose, but I'd ignored them, determined to find my true family, and I had uncovered a monster who would kill me. 'Then his mind will really be at rest.'

'Oh, no, James.' She looked shocked. 'He wouldn't wish you any harm.'

I stared at her. This was the man who had caused the death of Eddie Quennell, who had been her close friend—perhaps she had even loved him—and yet she went on believing that Lord Rivers was a gentleman with decent instincts. How could she?

'You'll think it's strange,' Mrs Hailstone said, 'but these are not bad people at heart, James. I know them, I've lived in their house for twenty years. They find themselves pushed by things that don't concern people like you and me. One mistake, and they have to make another.'

'No, they don't.' I was too angry and upset to listen to excuses, and I could never understand why servants had such a respect for their masters. 'If we're supposed to behave decently, then so are they.'

Mrs Hailstone gave a small shrug, and changed the subject. 'What are you going to do, James?'

Red Jack, I thought. I seemed to be reaching for him like a drowning person struggling towards a rock. 'I must find out who killed Mr Quennell and my friend. It could be two different people, but that doesn't matter. There's someone who might help. A coster.'

She nodded. 'I know who you mean. If I can help, I will. I caused all this, you see, because of what I did all those years ago. I feel responsible—to Eddie.' Tears came again. 'I loved him, you see.' She struggled for a moment, then composed herself. 'My husband died very soon after we were married. I was very lonely. There had been trouble in my family because they hadn't approved of the marriage. And Eddie was so kind. We always thought we'd find a little house in Dover one day—my sister lives down there. But you won't want to hear all this.'

I leaned forward and said, 'It wasn't your fault. Eddie didn't have to write that letter, he chose to. And—I want to thank you for what you did. Poll, who brought me up—she's been great. The sort of mother anyone would want.'

'I'm glad,' said Mrs Hailstone. But her mind had jumped back to the question that bothered her, and she added, 'Lord Rivers wasn't to know that you'd be suspected of Eddie's murder, James. I'm sure he'll do what he can to clear things up. After all, you are a blood relative, even though you can't be publicly recognized.'

I wasn't impressed. 'What about my father?' I asked. 'Is he one of Lord Rivers's friends as well?' I hardly wanted to know any more.

'Miss Judith would never say. There was a young Guards officer, but I don't know.' Mrs Hailstone pondered. 'He and Miss Judith used to go riding in the park together—she was mad about horses. There was always a chaperone with her, though. I used to go myself sometimes, though I never liked riding. Miss Judith was a wonderful horsewoman, always in the stables, making

sure the animals were properly cared for. She was a bit of
a tomboy. Such a lovely girl, though.'

'What happened afterwards?' I asked. 'Did she get
married?' Maybe I had half-brothers or sisters.

'Yes. A brilliant match, everyone said, to Lord
Pembleton. He's a lot older than her. I never thought he
was a suitable husband.'

'Did they have children?'

'No. You were her only one. Poor Miss Judith.' Mrs
Hailstone sighed. 'She wanted to be a teacher, you
know—she often talked to me about it. But the family
wouldn't have it, of course.'

'Why not?'

'Well-brought-up girls are not supposed to work. It's
part of a gentleman's pride, you see, that he has enough
money to keep a wife and a proper household. She gives
lectures, though,' she added. 'Every Tuesday evening, at
the Drapers' Hall.'

'Lectures?' I didn't know what the word meant.

'Talks. About literature. Shakespeare, Milton, all that.'
Then she stood up. 'I must go. Roper will be locking the
house for the night.'

I stood as well, and she gripped my hand tightly. 'Be
careful James. Don't come here again. If there's any news,
I'll hear.'

I wondered how, but I didn't ask her. The odd-coloured
eyes stared briefly into mine, then she turned and walked
away.

16

'So that's what you've been up to,' said Red Jack, surveying my dishevelled dress and slipping shawl. 'Are you off your head, boy? It's not safe, running round London like that.'

'I know,' I said. I'd had a bit of bother in an alley with a well-dressed man who stepped from a doorway to grab me and fumble at my skirts. I'd had to resort to a swift kick and a knee in the groin, then I'd run for it.

'You heard about young Luke?'

I nodded.

'Sit down, boy.' We were in his back room, with the light glinting on the porcelain figures as if nothing in the fierce outside world could disturb this warmth and brightness.

'It's all because of me,' I said. 'What happened when I was born. I found out.' And I told him what Poll had said, and then about Mrs Hailstone.

At the end of it, Red Jack nodded, and I had the feeling he wasn't entirely surprised. 'That fits,' he said. 'Fits very nicely.'

'But what can I do? Mrs Hailstone says Lord Rivers wouldn't mean me any harm, but—'

'I wouldn't be sure of that,' said Red Jack. 'You've done quite enough, Joey. You're going to stay here until this is sorted out. Your unfortunate friend came to see me last night—did you know that?'

'No. He said he would, but I wasn't sure.'

'We had a word with this Togger Bill he spoke of—

works on the night-cart. He was very helpful.' Red Jack smiled a satisfied, tom-cat smile.

'Was it him, then?' I was startled. Lucky hadn't been at all sure.

'Oh, no. But he's going to be a very useful witness.'

'Witness?'

'At the trial.' Red Jack smiled again. 'Not what you're thinking, boy. None of your lawyers and wigs. This'll be a costers' trial. It's a few years since we've had one.'

I nodded. I'd heard of the makeshift courts that sorted out quarrels or brought a ruling against a coster who'd been making a nuisance of himself. But this was something bigger. 'When's it going to happen?' I asked.

'Tomorrow night,' said Red Jack. 'Word's gone round. And I don't want you leaving here until it's over.'

'But I'm staying with Pocky Dan and Kate, they'll be wondering—'

'I'll let 'em know. You hungry?'

I was ravenous, as usual, and Red Jack got up and went to the door of the outer room. 'Dorrie,' I heard him say, 'find this lad something to eat, will you?' His voice was casual and pleasant, but he sounded like a man who does not expect to be disobeyed.

Lying on the leather sofa with an old horse-blanket over me, with no light now except the glow of the dying fire, I could not sleep, even though I was comfortably full of cold beef and fried potatoes. Images jostled in my mind for attention—Lucky Luke walking away down the street, Rose close to me in the shop doorway, Mrs Hailstone's gripped hands in their mended grey gloves, and then the man who had grabbed me in the alley. I understood for the first time how bad it was for a girl to be overpowered and have taken from her by force that which should be given in love—and I wondered whether my own birth was the result of some such assault. But surely that was exactly why the daughters of the gentry were so carefully protected? It seemed more likely that Miss Judith had looked kindly on the man who had become my father, and given herself to him in secret love and willingness. I hoped so. There was enough violence in my new-found family without a girl's violation as well.

Most of all, I thought about the trial. By this time tomorrow night, it would be over. But then what? Red Jack had refused to tell me any more, but a trial meant a man must be tried—and who was that? If the costers had by some miracle found the true culprit, and the trial proved him guilty, what would happen? In a proper court of law, sentence would be passed and the guilty man would be hanged. Surely Red Jack could not have an executioner waiting to do his grisly job?

And even if he did, my mind went on, *where would I stand then?* The costers could decide what they liked, but until the police knew for a fact that someone else had killed Quennell, and Lucky, too, they would go on looking for me. What about Meachum and his paid army of faceless men? What about my own grandfather, who sat like a spider in the centre of this terrible web? Even when I slept, my mind was full of uneasy dreams.

Dorrie was nudging me. 'There's coffee on the table,' she said, 'and some bread. Pa says you've to stay here and not go out. There's some ham in the cupboard if you get hungry, midday. And if you're not busy, you could sort some potatoes for me. There's two sacks by the wall in the other room.' She, too, spoke as if she didn't expect any argument, but I didn't mind. I certainly wasn't going to be busy.

Red Jack had left Quennell's book on the table. It seemed to have come from a lost, remembered time, like the things in Poll's treasure box. I wiped my fingers carefully when I had finished eating and turned the pages one by one. Then I put it aside as a treat to be savoured later, and set about Dorrie's potatoes, dropping the rotten ones into a bucket. I carried this downstairs and tipped it out on the midden, washed my hands under the pump, then came back and locked the door.

Hours passed as I murmured my way through the words I knew and went on to work out the sound and meaning of less familiar ones. With Quennell's lost voice somewhere in my ear, I was so greedy to learn that I didn't get up to look for the ham in Dorrie's cupboard, but as the winter light began to fade, sleepiness swam over me in a great wave, and I put my head down on my arms and slept.

A rattling at the locked door woke me, and Dorrie's whisper—'Joey! Let us in.'

She'd brought a big slab of plum-cake to share out among the children who had come in with her, and she gave me a slice as well. Then she said, 'You'll need proper clothes for tonight. Pa said we'd to find you something.' She looked at her eldest boy and added, 'You're not that different in size. Walter, go and get your spare shirt.'

It was a bit short in the arms, but it didn't show under a jacket belonging to Dorrie's husband, Bert, who was a bulky man. A pair of his cast-off trousers had to be bunched in with a bit of rope round the waist because there wasn't a spare belt, but with a waistcoat over the shirt and a red and blue kingsman knotted at my neck, I felt like a coster again.

Red Jack came in just as we were sitting down to smoked haddock and potatoes. He looked tired, and pulled his chair to the table in silence. None of his family asked him any questions or said anything about what lay ahead of us this evening, and I had the feeling that they wouldn't get an answer even if they'd tried it. I was glad when Bert said, 'How are we going to get Joey up there?' It was a thing I'd been worrying about myself, knowing that the police would be on me like a flash if I walked through the streets undisguised.

'In the barrow,' Red Jack said. 'A couple of the kids can ride in it, and we'll put some sacks over Joey.'

Bert nodded and said, 'I'll go and harness Queenie.'

'Wait till it's darker.' Then the big man turned to me. 'Stand up, let's have a look at you.' His fox-brown eyes inspected my clothes. 'You need a belt. I'll get you one.' He went into his room and returned with a handsome leather belt with brass eyelets. 'That's more like it.'

'Where are we going?' I asked. 'I mean, where's the trial happening?'

'In a warehouse near Bishopsgate. Along the end of Sun Street.'

'What do I have to do?' I was beginning to feel very nervous.

'Just answer what I ask you. Stick to the facts, right? No guesswork.'

'Who's going to be there?'

Red Jack smiled briefly. 'Everyone,' he said.

In the barrow, I was covered by more than sacks. A half-load of cabbages was tipped on top of me, and whenever they tended to roll aside, the children pushed them back with their feet. It seemed a long ride, but nobody stopped us, and at last the donkey called Queenie came to a halt. 'Right,' Red Jack said. 'Everyone out.'

In the light of the moon that stood above gaping rafters, I saw that most of the houses in the street had been demolished, giving way to a wide field of rubble, though on the other side the warehouse still stood. It was tall and flat-fronted, and most of its windows were broken. Red Jack pushed the door open, and we walked into a vast, shadowy space. Lamps hung from beams above a makeshift platform, and crates and boxes had been put in a rough half-circle facing it. A lot of people were already there, and Rose emerged from the crowd with Meg and Stevie at her heels.

I put my arms round her, and it seemed as if the two of us were the only thing that was real. Everything else was just a nightmare that had worked its way into waking life, where it didn't belong.

Meg reached up to touch my arm. 'Are you coming home tonight?' she asked, and Stevie watched, serious and frowning.

'I hope so,' I said. And if I'd known a bit more about God, I might have prayed that my wish would be granted.

I was going to go and sit down with Rose, but Red Jack stopped me. 'I want the witnesses up here,' he said. 'By the platform.' Some big packing cases screened off a shadowed place where several men were already waiting, and I went to join them. I didn't know who any of them were. I thought of the penny gaffs where actors waited in the wings, and felt even more bemused. I'd never thought I would play a part in a theatre, specially one as frightening as this.

From my hidden place, I spotted the baker and his wife, and saw with relief that Quennell's thin little dog was with them, wearing a smart leather collar and a lead held by Mrs Jarrett.

Poll came in with a tall coster at her side, and for a stupid moment I was startled that it wasn't Curly. I watched them go across to a box and sit down, and saw

Poll smile up at Lanky Phil as he released an edge of her shawl that had caught on a splinter, and was moved by a strange pity for all the years she had spent with a man who could give her nothing but roughness. Curly had loved her—I was sure of that—but only as a man loves all the things he needs and enjoys. I hoped I'd never think of Rose in that way. But then, of course, Rose would never let me.

The heavy door opened again, and two costers came in, escorting between them a skinny man whose wrists were bound in front of him with rope. He wore a blue coat and smart black boots, but he was so scared that his legs seemed barely able to carry him. The costers were at least half a head taller than him and held him by an arm apiece, hustling him towards the dark space where I stood. He didn't look at me or show any sign of recognition, but when I saw his limping gait, his pinched nose, and rheumy, red-rimmed eyes, I knew at once who he was— the man who had tried to borrow twopence from me at the doss-house. Johnny Pink.

17

I watched as the warehouse gradually filled up, hoping that Kate and Dan would come, but there was no sign of them. They weren't costers, of course, so perhaps this didn't concern them, but I wished they'd been there.

The place was buzzing with talk, but everyone quietened as Red Jack mounted the platform, and the sea of faces turned towards him attentively.

'You know why we're here,' he said. 'Last week, a man called Edward Quennell, known as Quill Quennell, was killed in his room above Jarrett's baker's shop in Middlesex Street. The police have reason to think a coster boy called Joey, from Sugarloaf Court, committed this crime, but he says he didn't. The purpose of this trial is to find out the truth of what happened.'

Heads turned as the door opened again, and to my astonishment, Mrs Hailstone came in, accompanied by a lean man in a black hat and coat—Sammy Meyer. There was a mutter of surprise from the crowd, but Red Jack went across to the oddly-assorted pair as if he had been expecting them. 'Thank you both for coming,' he said. A glance at a couple of costers was enough to set them moving boxes so that Sammy and Mrs Hailstone could sit down near to where I stood, but people were still staring and murmuring. Mrs Hailstone was completely unknown to them, but equally startling was the presence of Sammy. We got on all right with the Jews and respected them for the way they drove a hard bargain but stuck to their word, but they kept their affairs to themselves and so did we, and Sammy's presence here was a mystery.

'As I was saying,' Red Jack went on, 'a coster boy is suspected of killing Quennell, and possibly of another murder as well. A lad known as Lucky Luke was found dead yesterday morning.' He turned his head and looked at me. 'Joey, will you come up here, please.'

I stepped onto the platform and walked towards him. My legs didn't seem to belong to me and my mouth felt dry.

The fox-brown eyes looked into mine. 'When did you first meet Quill Quennell?'

Answering his questions, I went through the whole story of the doss-house, my reading lessons, the final evening when the little dog, Sadie, had disappeared, and Mrs Jarrett's accusation the following morning when Quennell's death had been discovered. Red Jack didn't ask about anything else, just nodded and said that would do. 'Now let's hear from Mrs Jarrett.'

The baker's wife handed Sadie's lead to her husband and came up.

'What exactly did you see on the night when Quill Quennell was killed?' Red Jack asked.

'I saw young Joey walking across the street from our door. Bold as brass he was.'

'What do you mean, "bold"?'

'Well—like he could take his time. He had something under his arm. A book, it looked like.'

'And he was taking his time,' Red Jack said. 'Not running, then. Not looking scared or furtive?'

'Oh, no.' Then she frowned as people took the point and laughed. 'He could have pinched the book, couldn't he? Knifed Mr Quennell for it?' She was losing confidence, and the crowd booed and cat-called.

116

Red Jack held up his hand for silence, then turned to me again. 'What about this book, Joey?'

I explained, and Red Jack nodded. Then he asked, 'Did Quennell say anything about feeling he was in danger? Was he reckoning he might not see you again?'

'No—we'd arranged I'd come for a lesson the next day.'

'Did he seem worried about anything?'

'He was worried about his dog. She'd gone missing, and he didn't have the money to pay if someone asked a reward for bringing her back.'

There was a mutter of disapproval. Nobody liked the dog-finders.

'What did you do when you left him?'

'I went to try and find Lucky Luke. I thought he might have the dog.' I didn't want to talk about Lucky now he was dead, but I had no choice. 'He was in that business.'

'Did you find him?'

'Not that night. But I ran into him two days ago, the evening before he was killed.' I wasn't sure if Red Jack wanted to go into all that, but he nodded encouragingly. 'Go on,' he said.

I repeated what Lucky had told me about finding Quennell dead when he brought the dog back, and about the man who had been in the room, and a slow mutter came from the crowd.

Red Jack hushed them again. 'What happened then?'

The meeting in the dark alley was still sharp in my mind—I could feel the bonnet ribbons under my chin and hear Lucky's brave, scared voice. 'He said if he'd been seen by the man in the room, he might be for it himself. And I said we needed help.'

'So you sent him to me,' said Red Jack.

'Yes.'

He reached across to the packing-case beside him, and

picked up a sheet of paper. 'I wrote down what he told me, and he put his mark when I read it back to him, agreed that was what he'd said.' He held up the sheet of paper, and everyone gazed respectfully at the lines of neat writing, and the bold cross and thumb-print at the bottom. I wondered why I'd never realized that the big man could read and write.

Mrs Jarrett looked unconvinced. 'He could have been lying,' she said. I almost smiled at her sudden changing of sides, but Red Jack just looked at her. 'I don't often get lied to,' he said. He read out Lucky's statement, which ended with his suggestion that the man behind the door could have been Togger Bill, then laid the paper down carefully. 'Let's have Togger Bill,' he said. 'And his mates.'

The men who were ushered out looked very clean and well-scrubbed, and one of them leaned heavily on a stick and had to be helped onto the platform. This, it turned out, was Togger Bill. He answered Red Jack's questions reluctantly. Yes, they had been in Aldgate High Street that night. Yes, Jarrett's shop was visible from the crossroads. No, they didn't go up Middlesex Street, the houses didn't have modern plumbing with sewage tanks in the basement.

'And did any of you leave the cart at that time?'

It was the leader of the group, a man with a gingery moustache, who answered. 'How could we? It takes all five of us to do our job. Togger drives the cart, I go into the houses with a long rod, stir the stuff in the tanks—it's important, that, else you only get the liquid off the top— then young Alf lets the bucket down and hauls it up full. Les and Percy empty it into the cart. It's a big bucket. Heavy work.'

I wondered why Red Jack was bothering with all this. Togger Bill's right leg was so twisted that only the toe of his boot touched the ground. It was obvious that he couldn't have got off the cart without some help, let alone climb the steep stairs to Quennell's room. Lucky must have known him some time ago, before he got so disabled, or he'd never have suggested him. Togger was explaining his injury to Red Jack.

'It was a dislocated hip,' he said. 'I couldn't afford doctoring so it never got put back. I could get about up to a year or so ago, but it was getting worse. I had to give up the second-hand clothes trade, couldn't carry a pack any more. Got myself a job on the cart.'

'And you start work at about ten o'clock at night, when there aren't many people about,' said Red Jack. 'Sitting on the driver's seat, you'll have a good view all round, though. Did you see anyone come out of Middlesex Street that night?'

Togger Bill frowned. 'Could have done,' he said.

'Come along,' said Red Jack gently. 'You can do better than that. Did you see anyone?'

'Well, yes.'

'Where?'

'He came out of a shop in Middlesex Street, down towards us. Crossed over the High Street in front of the cart. I don't know where he went after that.'

'Was it the baker's shop?'

'Yes.'

'What did he look like?'

Togger's frown deepened. 'Skinny bloke. Limped a bit—not as bad as me, though.'

'And was he going slowly because of this limp?'

'No. He was going along as fast as his legs would carry him.'

Red Jack gave a nod to the costers who waited by the rough screen that hid the waiting witnesses—though I knew there was only one left now—then turned back to Togger Bill.

'Would you know this man if you saw him again?'

'I might,' Togger said reluctantly.

The costers brought out Johnny Pink, almost lifting him onto the platform. They had untied his wrists, and the skinny man stood rubbing them. Everyone saw the way he limped—and they saw, too, the expensive new boots and the blue coat. 'How much did you get paid?' someone shouted amid derisive laughter.

Red Jack held up his hand. Then he asked, 'Is this the man you saw?'

'Could be,' said Togger.

'IS IT?' roared Red Jack, so suddenly that everyone jumped and Togger Bill visibly flinched.

'Yes,' he said.

'You're sure?'

'Yes.' Wretchedly, he glanced at Johnny Pink and muttered, 'Sorry, mate.'

I wondered what Red Jack had said to make the night-cart man give evidence. *We had a word with Togger Bill.* Who had he meant by 'we'? I remembered again the rumours that people were found floating in the river, and a chill ran down my spine. Johnny Pink and Togger Bill had both been in the old-clothes trade—they knew each other. I saw Johnny look back at the man who had betrayed him. 'Doesn't matter,' he said. 'Best if it's over quickly.'

Suddenly I noticed that Quennell's dog, which had been lying quietly beside Mr Jarrett, had got up and was straining against her lead as she leaned forward, staring at Johnny Pink. Her legs were trembling and her ears flat against her head, and she began to growl, then burst into a torrent of snarling and barking.

Mrs Jarrett stared as her husband tried to calm the dog. 'Funny,' she said, 'she's such a quiet little thing. Never made a sound since we've had her.' Then she looked at Johnny Pink, and realized when Sadie had last seen him, and put her hand to her mouth. 'Oh, my God,' she said.

Bedlam broke out at this fresh proof that Johnny Pink was the man who had been in Quennell's room. 'String him up!' someone shouted, and there were yells of agreement.

Red Jack faced the crowd. *This is a trial, not a lynch mob,'* he bellowed at them. 'So give the man a chance to be heard, right?' When they were quiet, he turned to me. 'Joey, do you know this man?'

'Yes.' I told him about the doss-house in Scarborough Street where Johnny had tried to make Quennell let him in cheap, and about his attempt to borrow money from me, and Red Jack nodded.

'What was he wearing at the time?'

'Scruffy old stuff. He was going to sleep in the kitchen.'

'So he was skint. Did you see anyone else you knew at this doss-house?'

I frowned, thinking of the bare-foot Irishwoman and the two little boys who shared a bed—then saw what he meant. 'Meachum came to collect the money from Quennell,' I said.

There was a roar at the mention of Meachum's name, and while it was going on, Red Jack stepped off the platform and went over to Mrs Hailstone. He escorted her back with him, and the crowd quietened in curiosity. She turned her white face to look at me, and I found my palms sweating. This was where the whole story of my birth would come out. She could not explain Quennell's blackmail attempt without referring to it—and where would I be then? Lord Rivers's long-kept secret would be blown wide open, and sooner or later, Meachum and his spies would hear about it and convey the news back to their master. Mrs Hailstone had said he meant me no harm, and she obviously believed it, or she would not have come here. There was a risk to herself as well, but perhaps with her beloved Eddie gone, she did not care.

The warehouse was very quiet as Red Jack began his questioning.

'Your name is—?'

'Mrs Hailstone. Kathleen.'

'And you have a job?'

'I am housekeeper for Lord Rivers.'

Steadily, she went through the whole story of the child who was born and given away and of Quennell's hope that he could make money through a threat to expose this secret. She did not mention my name, but heads turned in my direction, and a few people grinned. Then Red Jack voiced the question that had come to my mind so often since my meeting with Mrs Hailstone.

'How did you know of Poll? Were you born here?'

'No. But my husband was. He—' For the first time, she faltered, and her eyes sought out Sammy. He got up and came to the platform.

'As most of you know, I am Samuel Meyer,' he said, 'from Houndsditch. Wholesale fruit. This lady married my brother-in-law, Isaac Holstein.' There was a buzz of interest and some disapproval, and he waited for it to subside. 'Her family cut her off for marrying a Jew, and many of my own family, I am sorry to say, did not accept Kathleen for the same reason in reverse—she was a *shiksa*—a Gentile. Within a year of the marriage, Isaac died—he was never strong as a boy. My wife and I liked Kathleen, and we took her in until she found herself this live-in job as a housekeeper. During that time, she had applied for several posts and been turned down without so much as an interview, and I said to her that she should change her name. Many of us have to do this if we need to be accepted by the English gentry. So Holstein became Hailstone, and she was taken on by Lord Rivers. But we kept in touch with Kathleen, and helped her when we could.'

Sammy's eyes met mine, and he gave me a small smile. So he had known all along who I was, I thought. And I had just thought he was a decent Jewish trader who would always give me a break.

Red Jack was probing for more information about Lord Rivers.

'He is a shipping magnate,' Mrs Hailstone said. 'He owns a fleet of passenger liners, and trading ships as well, that go all over the world. China, Africa, America.'

China, I thought. Where the opium poppies grew. I saw now how it was that Meachum had a cheap supply.

'When this threat came from Quennell, Lord Rivers couldn't go to the police,' Red Jack said. 'So he took care of it privately?'

'Yes.' Mrs Hailstone's voice was barely audible.

'So who did he turn to?'

'His lawyer. Ellis Meachum.'

Howls of derision broke out, and went on as Red Jack took Sammy and Mrs Hailstone back to their places. Mrs Jarrett rejoined her husband and the night-cart men sat down, leaving nobody on the platform but me and Johnny Pink with his guards.

Red Jack stepped up to join us, and turned to face the still noisy audience. 'Right,' he bellowed. 'We're going to hear from Johnny Pink now. And if anyone interrupts him or makes a row, I'll have him thrown out.'

Nobody doubted that he meant it.

Johnny Pink, shoved forward by the costers, sniffed and rubbed his nose on the sleeve of his blue coat. 'I wish I'd never set eyes on him,' he said.

'On who?' asked Red Jack.

'Meachum. And Quennell, too. It was at the doss-house, see. After the accident.'

'You'll have to start at the beginning,' Red Jack said patiently. 'What accident was this?'

'Down at the knacker's yard, about two years ago. I used to work there—slaughterman.' He rubbed his nose again and began to get into his stride. 'A horse reared up sudden when I was putting the blindfold round its eyes. We always did that, so they didn't see what was going to happen. But this one went wild, knocked me flat, trampled all over me. Smashed the bones in my foot, broke my ribs. I got inflammation of the lungs, nearly died.'

Everyone listened in silence.

'I had to give my room up, of course—couldn't pay for it. The people upstairs took me in, they were real good to me. But I couldn't stay there, they'd four children, there wasn't space. I begged for a bit, while I was still on crutches, then when I could get around a bit better I started in the old-clothes trade. Togger Bill helped me set up. I was living in the doss-house. I knew there was narks who got a free bed for a bit of checking-up, like, and I thought I could do that. I had a word with Quennell. He used to take the money, he knew me. He said he'd ask. Well, that was the start of it.'

'Of what?' Red Jack asked.

'Little jobs. Nothing much at first—carrying letters, waiting for an answer. But it got worse. I'd to loosen the axle-pin in a carriage. That was going to be a nasty accident for someone. I lamed horses. I hated doing that. Knackering's one thing, but I don't like mucking them about.'

'You could have said no,' someone shouted, and Pink gave a slight shake of his head.

'I daren't. I tried it once, when I was asked to set a place on fire. Quennell looked at me and said did I know

124

what I was saying. I said I did—but that night, a couple of blokes shoved me into a dark alley and put a knife to my throat. I was free to choose, they said. Do the job or die. So I did it.'

'But you were being paid,' said Red Jack.

'Yes. I'd moved out of the doss-house by this time. Got a room of my own, better than I'd ever dreamed of. But the orders kept coming. It was never Meachum himself, nor Quennell either. Some man would turn up—I never knew when.'

Red Jack's next question sounded almost casual. 'And did you kill Quennell?'

The crowd held its breath, and in the utter silence, Johnny Pink said, 'Yes, I killed Quennell. And I'll regret it as long as I live.'

'That won't be long!' someone shouted, and yells and jeers broke out, though other people were frowning and looking troubled.

'*Quiet!*' Red Jack roared. He turned back to the drooping figure before him and asked, 'Did you also kill Lucky Luke?'

'No.' Pink looked up with a pathetic effort at bravery. 'If they came, I was going to tell them I wouldn't. I knew it would be the end, but I didn't care. Quennell—I couldn't get it out of my mind, it was like I was haunted. When you came, you and your men, I thought it was orders, and I was going to be killed for saying no.' He gave a helpless shrug. 'It doesn't matter. I'm done for.'

'You'd told someone you saw Lucky come into Quennell's room?' Red Jack enquired.

'Yes.' Again Pink sniffed and rubbed his sleeve across his face. 'The bloke that brought the money. He asked if it had gone all right, and I was that shaken, I said what had happened.'

There was another hiss and mutter from the crowd. Red Jack waited for quiet, then asked, as if in polite interest, 'How much were you paid?'

'Five pounds,' said Pink.

This time, the warehouse erupted into shouts of derision and disgust. Red Jack let the noise go on for a few moments, then held up his hand.

'By all the evidence and by his own confession,' he said, 'Johnny Pink killed Quennell. We don't yet know about Lucky Luke, but that's a separate question. We have to decide now what to do with the man before us.'

'String him up!' the same voice yelled again, and uproar broke out, with people shouting their agreement or dissent. Then Poll stood up. All this time, I had been watching as if in a dream, standing on the platform as if I was merely a piece in a game, but as her eyes met mine, I was myself again, excited by the thought that I was actually going to be free.

'We are not murderers,' Poll said. 'And neither would Johnny Pink have been, if he'd had any choice. Let him go.'

There were mingled shouts from the crowd.

'What'll he do for another five pounds?'

'No, let him go—someone else will kill him.'

Lanky Phil was on his feet. 'Poll's right,' he said. 'It's not Johnny Pink we should be worrying about, it's the men behind him. They're the real killers. Pink's finished. We should let him go.'

Red Jack nodded agreement. His face was sombre, but intent. 'Put it to the vote,' he said. 'Who's for letting Johnny Pink go?'

After some hesitation, a slow forest of hands rose.

'Those against?'

Other hands went up, but everyone could see they were fewer.

'The decision of this court is clear,' Red Jack said. He turned to the cowering man before him and said, 'Johnny Pink, you are free to go.'

We all watched in silence as Pink limped towards the door. The costers standing there opened it for him—and a collective gasp ran through the crowded warehouse. There, in the dark doorway, stood Meachum.

18

Johnny Pink stumbled and almost fell, and Meachum stepped forward into the lamplight, reaching out a gloved hand to support him. 'Take your time, Mr Pink,' he said. 'There's no hurry.'

In the utter silence, there was something dreamlike about the way his silk-lined cloak fell back from his arm as he released the man and gestured to the open door. 'Please,' he said.

Everyone in the warehouse watched Johnny Pink as he blundered on—but Red Jack and I, standing on the platform, were the first to see the ring of policemen step forward from the darkness.

Johnny screamed like a rat when the dogs close on it. Nobody moved except Red Jack, who walked across the platform to meet the approaching Meachum. There was a heavy lack of surprise about his set face and the deliberation of his tread, and my thoughts turned a terrible somersault. In that moment, I was sure the whole thing was pre-arranged. Meachum's face held no triumph, only a solid satisfaction at a deal concluded. And Red Jack? I stared at the big man's back as he stood at the platform's edge, and wondered. My freedom would have meant nothing without this outcome. The police had to have their man. Lord Rivers knew that.

The implications dizzied me. Why would Meachum agree to throw his own man to the wolves? But when I thought of Johnny Pink's story, I saw that he had no real proof that Meachum was involved. His contact had been through Quennell, who was dead. Meachum could laugh at the suggestion that he had anything to do with it. I began to wonder myself if our suspicions had run away with us—and then I saw Mrs Hailstone's pale face, staring at the man in a white cravat with bitter hatred. She, perhaps, knew more than any of us, because of what Quennell had told her, and I feared for her.

The police had come into the warehouse, and were moving among the people, taking names. One of them was speaking to Red Jack, and they came across the platform towards me. I nearly ducked and ran, not sure yet that I was out of danger, but Red Jack said, 'It's all right, boy. Just a word, that's all.'

I couldn't bring myself to look at the policeman's face. Bright buttons, open notebook.

'James Rivers, also known as Joey?'

'Yes.'

'You should have come to us in the first place, lad. It would have saved a lot of trouble.'

I risked a glance at him. He wasn't smiling, but my fear began to subside.

'We knew you didn't do it,' he went on. 'You were interrogated by one of our officers in Lower Thames Street shortly before Quennell was killed, and we know where you went after that.' He indicated Red Jack with a sideways nod of his head. 'And he says you spent the rest of the night there. All the same, though, you should have told us you reckoned Lucky Luke had Quennell's dog.'

'I didn't kill Lucky,' I said, frightened all over again. 'He was my friend, I—'

'We know that, too.' This time, the peeler did smile. 'You were in Goulston Court with Daniel Benson, Punch and Judy man. He came and told us. Brought his wife with him and all his kids. The station was full of 'em.'

The breath went out of me in a sort of grateful gasp,

but I didn't know what to say. It didn't seem to matter. The policeman turned away, and Red Jack glanced at me. 'All right?' he asked quietly.

'More than all right. It's—just amazing. Thank you.' It sounded stupidly inadequate. I saw Meachum turn and walk out of the door, and panic rose again. The game would start afresh now. And this time, everyone knew who I was. I turned to Red Jack and said, 'But it's still going on. Quennell was killed to shut him up, and so was Lucky. But the secret's out now. Lord Rivers—my grandfather—what will he do?' And what had he done?

Red Jack smiled, but his eyes were tired. 'Lord Rivers doesn't care what people like us know, boy,' he said. 'Poor old Quennell's mistake was to threaten to tell the old man's pals. The nobs. Rivers wouldn't like them to know about Miss Judith's little indiscretion, but us—we don't count.'

Mrs Hailstone came up as we were speaking, with Sammy behind her.

'You were very brave,' I said, and felt a wave of concern for her. If Meachum had been listening at the door, as he almost certainly had, he now knew about her connection with Quennell. She, if she chose, could be just as great a danger to Lord Rivers as he had been.

She gave a weary shrug. 'What does it matter?' she said. 'With Eddie gone, all I could do was tell what I knew, and hope it would help to stop this evil going any further.'

'But Lord Rivers—'

'Lord Rivers, poor man, has much to regret, and it's too late for him to do anything about it. He suffered a stroke early this morning, James. They say he may not live. If he does, he will be paralysed and unable to speak.'

I stared at her. How could she call him a poor man? He was my grandfather, but I felt ashamed of him.

Mrs Hailstone put her hand on my sleeve. 'He's an old man, James,' she pleaded.

I said, 'Being old is no excuse for being wicked,' and she sighed.

'He didn't mean to be wicked,' she said. 'He tried to be a kind man, and he often was. But he was brought up to think the making of money and holding of power are the important things in life, and when his own daughter threatened to ruin the respect he counted on from his friends, he had to do something about it. I should have realized how far he'd go, but I didn't.'

How strange servants were, I thought again. It was as though she was the responsible one, charged with making sure her master was protected from all unpleasantness. When that failed, this lion among men behaved as lions do, and she blamed herself rather than him. 'What will you do now?' I asked.

'I'm getting the night mail down to Dover, to my sister's. My box is packed, it's at Sammy's. Eddie left me all his books, you know,' she added. 'There wasn't much else, but I'll love to have those.'

'I'll see to it,' Sammy said. 'Trust me.'

'Oh, I do.' Then she looked anxious. 'What's the time? We must go.'

The Jarretts walked past at that point, joining the people who were drifting out, and Mrs Jarrett waved at me cheerfully and said, 'Best of luck, love!'

Sammy closed his eyes and shook his head. 'Short memory,' he said. 'She's been telling everyone she was sure you were going to hang.'

'I'm glad they've got Sadie, though,' said Mrs Hailstone. 'Eddie would have liked that. Goodbye, James. I hope things go well with you.'

'And you,' I said.

I went with them to the door, where Red Jack's donkey

stood dozing between her shafts, and watched the pair of them go off down what was left of the street, her arm through Sammy's. Then I turned back and came face to face with Poll and Lanky Phil.

'Joey,' said Poll. 'Oh, Joey.' Her rough hands gripped my arms for a moment, then she groped in her coat pocket. 'Here. I should have let you take it that night when you came round. It's yours by rights.' And she put into my hand the folded letter with the small, rusted pin through its corner.

I put my arm round her shoulders and kissed her. There was too much to put into words. 'I'll come and see you soon,' I said.

'See us both,' Poll said. 'Phil's moving in with me.'

'I'm glad,' I said, and meant it.

They went out, and I turned to Rose, who had come to stand at my side. She held the sleeping Stevie in her arms. I took the little boy from her, happy to feel the relaxed weight of his body against my shoulder, and Meg slipped her hand into mine.

'Let's get home,' said Rose.

19

The next morning, I went up to Goulston Court to see Kate and Dan. I was still wearing the rather over-large clothes that Red Jack's family had lent me, and it seemed a very long time since I'd folded my own clothes and left them on a chair, walking out of Dan and Kate's room in the blue dress. People grinned as I walked through the market in Middlesex Street with my empty shallow over my shoulder, and someone called out, 'Best of luck, Joey!'

I'd need it, I thought. Last night's events had left me uneasily aware that the game went on—a vast game that involved money I couldn't imagine. What was the value of an entire ship's hold full of fruit and spices and the compressed essence of opium poppies that looked like putty? Even if the power of my grandfather had ended in paralysis and helplessness, there were other players, and as the lesser men like Meachum wriggled their way into a share of their wealth, the game reached out to touch people like me and Lucky. There were thousands of us, quite safe as long as we went quietly on with our grubby little lives—but heaven help us should we become an inconvenience.

Was I still an inconvenience? The question nagged at me—but it was so good to walk free, with a pale yellow winter sun shining in a clear sky, that I didn't care if this day was my last. Larks sang in their wicker cages as I passed the bird-catcher's stall, and for two pins I'd have let them all out to fly their sweet way.

Dan opened the door with a big smile. 'I hear you're a free man!' he said. 'Great news!'

'Coffee's brewing,' said Kate. 'The children have gone out for bread. It's such a nice morning, the lot of them went.'

'That'll mean a late breakfast,' Dan said. 'You know what they're like. They get playing hopscotch with their friends, eating the ends off the loaves, and we get what's left.'

'You're only young once,' said Kate. 'But what about you, Joe—tell us all about it.'

I poured out the story of all that had happened since I last saw them, and as I talked about Mrs Hailstone and what she had told me, Dan's face grew strangely tense. He and Kate exchanged a long glance, and as my tale came to an end, she took his hand with a wry smile.

'So, my darling,' she said. 'It seems your chickens have come home to roost. At least, one of them has.' She was speaking to him as though the pair of them were alone in the room, and I felt faintly embarrassed. But there was another reason for my visit, more important than whatever Kate and Dan might be talking about. I fished in the pocket of the jacket that Dorrie had lent me, and produced the folded letter with its small pin in the corner. 'Poll gave me this,' I said. 'She kept it all these years, but she brought it to the trial last night—she said I could have it. It's from Miss Judith. My mother. Can you read it? Please!'

Kate put out her hand for the letter, and her eyes flicked quickly across the graceful writing. She bit her lip, then read the words aloud.

'This is James, but I call him Joey. May God guide and watch over him, my little clown who was born of love into a cruel world.'

I frowned, trying to make sense of it, and Dan turned to me and said gently, 'Do you see, Joe?'

I shook my head. A mad possibility was nagging at me, but I couldn't take it in. *My little clown.* Dan had never called me Joey because he said it was a clown's name. The clown in the Punch and Judy show was a joey. Why would Miss Judith know that? *Born of love.* I swallowed hard. No, it couldn't be.

Dan sighed. 'I'll tell you the story, Joe. I'd have told you years ago if I'd known, but there was a bit missing, and you've just found it. My ma and pa were in the Punch and Judy business, same as I am now, but they died of typhus when there was the big epidemic. I wasn't much older than you . . . So I kept on with the show, working the streets mostly, but sometimes I got asked to do a children's party in one of the big houses. And at one of them, there was this young lady. The party was for her little brother. She came up afterwards, wanted to know how I did the voices and all that.'

He held my eyes steadily. 'You'll know yourself, Joe, what it's like when you fall for a girl. She's in your mind all the time. It feels like she's the one thing that's always been missing.'

'We get the picture,' Kate said with dry humour.

Dan put his hand over hers and said, 'That's the way I feel about you, my love. Always will. But I was young at the time, and on my own. I never thought she'd look at me, her being the daughter of a great house and me being a Punch and Judy man—but she did. I wasn't a bad-looking bloke in those days—it was before I went down with the smallpox.' He indicated his pitted face. 'I used to hang round the stables at the back of the house, hoping to catch sight of her. The grooms used to laugh, they said I didn't have a chance. But she was often in the stables, she was keen on horses. And she did look at me, and I touched her hand. After that we were on fire for each other. We'd kiss in the harness room, and the grooms pretended they didn't know. And then came a day when there was nobody about.'

I could hardly breathe. 'She was—Miss Judith?'

Dan nodded. And in the next minute, I was in his big, rough embrace. 'All this time,' he said huskily. 'And I never knew I'd a fine, big son.' He turned to Kate, suddenly anxious, and put an arm round her shoulders as well. 'You don't mind, my love?'

'How could I mind?' The three of us were in a hugging group, then we fell back a little, shaking our heads and laughing. 'Who could mind about the birth of a baby?' said Kate. 'There's something wrong with people who think that's a disaster.'

I looked up at Dan's tufty fair hair, so near to the colour of my own, and said, 'I should have known.' I felt ashamed now of the number of times I had seen him and spoken to him with no more than an easy feeling of liking.

Maybe Dan was feeling the same, because he said, 'I've looked at you sometimes and wondered. But I'd nothing to go on.'

'Didn't you know I'd been born, then?'

Dan shook his head. 'The grooms told me there was a rumpus going on in the house, and they reckoned it was because Miss Judith was expecting. Turned out they were right—the housekeeper tipped them the wink. They said I'd better keep away. Lord Rivers was saying he'd shoot the man if he found out who it was. I felt terrible about it. Given half a chance, I'd have married Judy and looked after her with all the love in the world—but there wasn't half a chance. Then everything went quiet. I met one of the grooms in a pub about a year later, but he didn't know what had happened. Miss Judith hadn't been near the stables for months. But there was no baby in the house, he was sure of that. And the housekeeper had clammed up, wouldn't say a word. I thought maybe they'd made my Judy have one of those operations, to get rid of the baby. Girls can die of that.'

'So you never knew I'd been given to Poll?'

'Not a word,' said Dan.

'We're not costers, you see,' Kate put in. 'Not part of your world. And it's common enough for a woman to bring up someone else's baby. Our young Will isn't mine, he's my sister's, but she died when he was born.'

Footsteps and chattering voices sounded on the stairs, and the children came tumbling in with their loaves. I smiled to see that one of them did indeed have the end bitten off.

'We've just discovered something,' Dan said to them. 'Joe here is your big brother.'

'Go on?'

'That's great!'

'How do you know?'

'We found a letter,' said Kate. 'Put some knives on the table, Sarah, and the butter.'

'Are you going to help us with the show?' asked little Nancy.

I smiled at her and said, 'I don't think so. I'm a coster.' *But I don't have to be*, I thought. *I could be anything.* It was a dizzying thought.

'There's other shows as well as Punch and Judy,' said Dan. 'Some of the showmen write their own.'

'I can't write,' I said.

'Ma can,' said Sarah as she hacked slices off the loaf. 'She's teaching me, and the little ones are learning, too. It's not hard once you get the hang of it.' And she handed me a slice of bread, warm and fragrant. 'Help yourself to butter.'

Two days later, I turned into Middlesex Street and wondered what was wrong. Or right, perhaps. A sort of holiday seemed to have come over the place. Knots of people stood about, talking, and a man laughed as he turned to spit in the gutter. 'Serve him right,' he said.

I wondered what was going on. I'd been out since before dawn, selling the new season's oranges round the big houses in Bishopsgate—I was keeping well clear of Finsbury—and hadn't seen anyone to talk to. I joined a group of costers at a coffee stall and bought myself a mug of coffee and a slice of buttered bread.

'What d'you think of that, then, young Joey?' one of them asked. 'Great news, eh?'

I must have looked blank, because another one gave me a cheerful shove on the shoulder and said, 'Haven't you heard?'

'Heard what?'

'Meachum. They fished him out of the river this morning.'

'No!' I almost spilt my coffee. *Red Jack*, I thought. *Red Jack*. Fox-brown eyes gleamed in my mind for a moment, then were replaced by the costers' grinning faces.

'That's stopped *his* gallop,' one of them said with satisfaction.

'Where—' I could hardly speak. 'Where did they find him?' I saw again the slipway down past the docks, and the rain-washed notice that said, PERSONS FOUND DROWNED.

'In the mud by Billingsgate. A kid came across him this morning. Face down, he was. And his hands were tied behind his back.'

I looked down at the slice of white bread in my hand. I'd folded it butter side inwards, ready to take a bite, but now I couldn't. *We are not murderers*, Poll had said. But somebody was. A murderer or an executioner. Was there a difference? Meachum had been a man with a lot of enemies, anyone could have killed him. Someone as desperate as Johnny Pink or someone with a power game

138

of his own. But there was something so neat about it. Billingsgate. Where Lucky had waved up to me from the mud as I sat on Curly's barrow all those years ago. And early this morning, some other boy, a mudlark like Lucky, had stumbled across the sodden bundle that had been a man.

I hoped there had been money in the pockets.

20

A week afterwards, Rose and I stood outside the Drapers' Hall in Throgmorton Street on a Tuesday evening. It was bitterly cold. Thin flakes of snow were starting to wander down, and Rose had her hands tucked under her arms, trying to keep warm. 'Wish she'd hurry up,' she said.

I felt guilty. 'We'll go home if you like,' I offered. 'Leave it for another week.'

Rose shook her head. 'We may as well stay now we've come. It can't be much longer. And you won't rest easy until you've seen her.'

She was right. The one thing that still stuck in my mind after all that had happened was the thought of Miss Judith. My mother. I wanted to see her, if only once. And Mrs Hailstone had said she gave these lectures on Tuesday evenings.

I hadn't known what time to come. The church clocks were striking a single note or half of their long chimes for half-past seven when we arrived, but the doors of the hall were already shut. Lights were on inside, though, and carriages waited in the courtyard, so we waited, too. As we watched, another carriage pulled up, and the driver climbed down from his box to throw rugs over the horses' backs. 'There'll be trouble if she thinks they're getting chilled,' he said to another driver. 'Her ladyship dotes on her horses like they were children.'

A few minutes later, the double doors of the hall opened and people began to come down the steps. A group stood in the doorway, centred round a tall woman who was tying the ribbons of a dark blue velvet cloak, and I felt suddenly breathless. This must be her. I couldn't get a proper view of her face because of the people who surrounded her.

'Wonderfully well done, Lady Pembleton,' a man was saying as he pulled on his gloves. 'I must read Pope again with fresh eyes.' And a woman in a feathered hat was gushing about what she called, 'An illuminating evening.' I wished they'd stop talking and move aside.

A maidservant handed Lady Pembleton her muff, and she slipped her hands inside it and moved forward a little. Her hair was almost as fair as Dan's, smoothly braided at the nape of her neck, and the smile she gave her admirers was a little sad, I thought. Or was I just expecting her to be sad? After all, this was Judy, as Dan called her. A girl who was full of life and love.

Rose slipped her hand into mine and gave it a little squeeze, and I was glad of that comfort as I went on gazing at the group in the doorway. The girl who had been Judy was gone now, though perhaps her ghost still lived somewhere in this slim woman who glanced down with approval at her waiting horses. She wore no hat, unlike the women round her, but she lifted the hood of her velvet cloak to cover her hair, and a liveried manservant stepped forward with an umbrella to escort her down the steps.

She paused as she saw Rose and me standing in the gutter, and fished in her purse for money. 'It's a terrible night,' she said. 'Here, take this.'

I couldn't move, but Rose held her hand out for the coins then dropped a curtsy, murmuring her thanks.

The woman's eyes met mine. Blue eyes under arched brows. Straight nose, wide mouth. We were not unalike. And with sudden, reckless courage, I said, 'I didn't come here for money.'

'Really?' The arched brows rose a little higher. 'Then why did you come, pray?'

'To see you.'

For a long moment, she stared at me through the falling snow. White flakes fell on the umbrella and on the maroon-clad arm of the man holding it. A faint flush came to her pale face, and her lips parted as if she was suddenly short of breath. Then a tactful cough came from the driver who was standing with the carriage door open, and she turned away. I watched her get into the carriage, followed by her maid. The driver shut the door, pulled the rugs off the horses and climbed up onto his box. Then he drove away.

The manservant shook his umbrella and folded it, then went back up the steps. The other carriages were departing, and the lights inside the hall were being extinguished.

Rose and I moved away as the last of the people dispersed. The snow was coming down heavily now, building up its whiteness in the streets so that the clatter of hooves and wheels was muffled into a soft thudding and rumble.

For a while we didn't speak, then Rose said, 'You nearly told her who you were, didn't you?'

'Nearly.' Had I been a coward? Angry confusion came over me, but it was partly because my boots were leaking. Having wet feet has always made me feel cross and miserable. But I'd get my boots mended next week if I put in another few days' good selling.

'You'd a right to tell her if you wanted,' said Rose. 'But it wasn't the right place. I was scared they'd give us in charge if you started anything. There were a couple of peelers just across on the corner.'

'I know.'

'You could write her a letter if you really wanted. Kate would help you. Only—'

I shook my head. Letters were dangerous. 'Too late,' I said. 'She gave up her baby so she could be what she has to be. I'm not that baby any more. Those years have gone, when I was small. She can't have them back. It would spoil everything if I turned up now. She'd have given me away for nothing.'

'That's what I thought,' said Rose. 'But I wanted to be sure you felt the same. Poor lady,' she added. 'I'm sorry for her. I'm glad we're not respectable.'

We walked on for a bit, then Rose said, 'Tell you what, though. When our baby's born, there's nobody going to make us give it away. It'll have a proper home with you and me.'

'*What?*' I stopped and stared at her, and she laughed at my astonished face. 'It'll be born next summer,' she said.

'But—why didn't you tell me?'

Rose shrugged. 'You might have decided to tell the lady the truth. I didn't think you would, but I couldn't be sure. Her family might have come round to the idea, specially now the old man's out of the picture. Sooner he dies the better, if you ask me. But I knew you'd stick by me if you knew about the baby coming, and I didn't want to twist your arm.' She looked up at me with her sparrow braveness. 'If you wanted to have a shot at being a toff, I wasn't going to stop you.'

'Oh, Rose. Dear Rose.' I stroked the melting snowflakes from her red hair and her freckled nose, and kissed her. Whatever else might happen, at least tonight I knew I had chosen right.

'Come on,' said Rose. 'We'll be warmer indoors.'

And we walked on through the familiar streets, that seemed so clean and new now in the freshly-fallen whiteness.

Other Oxford books

Hero
Catherine R. Johnson
ISBN 0 19 275197 2

Hero's father has been taken away to be sent back to the slave plantation, and Hero has been forced to move in with her mother's family in the East End of London. They despise Hero for being half black and the daughter of an escaped slave, and treat her as a skivvy and a prisoner.

But Hero's father was also a prizefighter, the best in the country, and Hero has inherited his fighting spirit. So when she decides to escape and rescue her father, she's ready to take on anyone who gets in her way . . .

The Coldest Winter
Elizabeth Lutzeier
ISBN 0 19 275202 2

Turned out of their home . . . their crops destroyed . . . too hungry to sleep . . . and cold to their very bones . . .

This is the story of Eamonn's struggle for survival. Can he keep himself and his family alive through the cold and the famine—through the coldest winter Ireland has ever known?

Bound for America
Elizabeth Lutzeier
ISBN 0 19 275167 0

Travelling to a new world—leaving behind the hunger and the hardship . . .

Eamonn knows that in America, land will be plentiful and there will be jobs for everyone. There, he'll be able to build a new life for his mother and his brothers, away from the bad times they've lived through in Ireland.

But will the reality live up to Eamonn's dreams? Or is there even more heartache in store?

Hold My Hand and Run
Margaret McAllister

ISBN 0 19 275168 9

Kazy has to save her little sister. The only way to do that is to run away, far from the abuse and beatings.

But they are being followed, searched for, chased. Can they avoid being taken home? Beth becomes seriously ill and the girls can't go on running any longer.

Beth needs help. But once you've run away, it's impossible to go back . . . isn't it?

War Song
James Riordan
ISBN 0 19 275192 1

The Girl Behind the Man Behind the Gun. That's what girls are told their role should be in the war. But Florence and Dorothy have other ideas. It's their war too, and they're determined to get in on the action.

So they both get involved—Dorothy in a munitions factory and Florence as a nurse. It's their big chance to do their bit—and to make something of their own lives, too.

But war is very real, whatever part you play in it. And before the fighting is over, the girls will have to find just as much strength as any soldier . . .